The Sarispa Thirteen

C.R. Coen

Aeonic Publishing

Cover design Slobodan Cedic

ISBN: *978-1-8382136-0-2*

To my daughters, your unwavering love and support, fills every breath with joy.

Table of Contents

Chapter One

Terrestrial Travel Only

Dharma boarded a standard terrestrial flight at Indira Airport, New Delhi. Reminiscent of a moving matchstick, she was showing real signs that she had the in-flight body swerve completely down—until she reached her seat. A solitary skinhead traveller loading luggage into the overhead locker knocked the back of her head. Dharma acknowledged an awkward apology and settled into her seat.

The aircraft moved into motion, assumed its position on the runway, and with a burst of speed, they were airborne. Fatigue claimed her. Through closed eyes, she heard in her mind the message that prompted her sudden, yet expectant journey. *Brodgar terrestrial travel only.*

Recalling the message awakened a visual recap of her previous twenty-four hours, which Dharma watched from the comfort of her flight seat. Through the window of her mind's eye, she saw the image of herself moving military style into a small, circular room, kneeling beside a basic bed, pulling out a ready-to-roll kit bag, boarding an awaiting helicopter and parting with Mount Kailaish.

'Intel on route.' The pilot had shouted over the whirring blades, barely landing on the makeshift heliport before taking off again.

Dharma and her unearthly shadow set off; the recall shot forward to the image of an old car parked in the shade of a Bodhi tree. The intergalactic traveller revved up a dust cloud, cranked up the music and drove.

The coordinates and a thirteen-hour drive took Dharma to Indira Airport. The visual download stalled, interrupted by cabin staff moving through the craft, offering refreshments. Dharma watched the man sitting opposite order enough food and water for the eight-hour flight and any potential return. She ordered water, took her change and caught a rush—a synchronistic flash that she hadn't seen in a long time.

'You're dehydrated and probably sleep deprived,' the man sitting opposite leaned in towards her. 'Rehydrate, then sleep.'

Dharma looked up and down the craft then back at the man. She knew what she had seen, and sleep would not be happening any time soon. Telepathic visions flooded her mind, crumpled-up mini-movies rolling into one. An unnatural flash of colour, normally from the eyes, is a sure sign that a Sarispa capable of dream-walking is within your close vicinity. Dharma scanned the passengers and crew onboard the craft, then turned to the man sitting opposite and took a closer look at him. Stepping deeper into her mind's eye, she became the conductor of her thoughts; gaining order and calm, she slowed down the visions and watched them one by one, but learned nothing about the man sitting opposite. What she could see and did know, she had company onboard the flight.

A skilled Sarispa walker is potentially quite hazardous. Those that can walk your dreams can gain knowledge of your deepest psyche, gathering valuable intel. Many ancient walkers hold dream-altering capabilities; if one's dreams are altered, it can cause chaos and wreak havoc within one's timeline and, indeed, one's existence. Dharma has the skills to block such attacks, but they generate an energy that's not particularly compatible with terrestrial aviation; not a risk she would be willing to take on a civilian flight.

In order to block a dream-walk attack, a dual stage of protection is required. Firstly, the intergalactic agent must induce a powerful shield around their physical being, which in itself can cause a violent turbulent reaction. The second step involves the agents stepping down into their timeline within the intergalactic matrix. Working within the matrix, another virtually impenetrable shield is placed around their actual being. The second step is the stage that can cause real problems onboard terrestrial aviation. Entire aircrafts have been known to disappear midflight, albeit momentarily. Catch the visual, if you will: one minute you're quite happy, sitting on a flight to Tenerife, the next minute, the plane disappears; you'll probably notice the craft a moment later as you fall, scream, and quite probably vomit through the clouds.

Having considered her options from a natural quantum perspective, she easily deduced she didn't have many alternatives. The fact the Federation had instructed her to travel via terrestrial methods was not unheard of—often an indication that the matrix is not a safe or advisable method of travel at that time. Her choices were limited, but she did have two. Remain under orders, stay awake and on route. With this option, she would have to create a scenario that would induce an explosive adrenal rush, something intense enough to carry her the remaining eight hours of the flight. The second option was to go to the restroom, exit the plane, and travel the remainder of the journey to Brodgar via the matrix.

Dharma stood up and took her bag out of the overhead compartment; the man opposite did a rapid double-take and perhaps an even faster stance.

'Can I help with that?' he asked, yet his action told another story as he pushed her bag back into the compartment.

'Quick freshen up,' she said, ignoring his motion, and she continued to drag the kit bag out of the locker. Setting off through the aircraft, he watched as she disappeared behind the toilet door.

Instant warmth grew in the cramped space. Dharma transformed her energy, and then the surrounding energy; it was an oil-and-water effect, no longer one but separate. The earthly looking intergalactic faded, effortlessly released from her present quantum existence. A supernova of light surrounded her, an infinite flow of electric blue energy engulfed her. Dharma and the matrix became one.

Chapter Two

The Ring of Brodgar

A standing stone circle on the Scottish island of Orkney awakened. A light danced an ancient dance with elegant knowing, and through the intimate interwoven flow, a mandala domed the standing stones and Dharma's hovering holographic form. The light and the hologram disappeared, the stone circle stood empty, and Dharma passed into the Intergalactic Federation's Brodgar C.I.T. base.

In vibrant contrast to the stark Orkney landscape, the subterranean base was more reminiscent of a flourishing progressive settlement. The only tangible similarities between the terra lands above and Earth's Hollow Kingdom below were mirrored in the stone circles—as above and so below. Standing in the circle for just a moment longer, the returning intergalactic breathed in the island. From her elevated position, Dharma watched the mesmerizing flow of oscillating waves wash against the island base. Sensing a call, she began to navigate her way down the hillside. Her kit bag became cumbersome as she worked her way through the exotic forest. Plants looked like animals, and the trees could quite probably house a small village. Hearing the hum of a hoverboard in the distance, the earthly looking intergalactic launched up a tree. She blended with her natural surroundings and scanned the area. Dharma spotted a kid, no older than ten, zip and trick his way through the forest.

'There you are, Dharma.' A feral-looking boy shouted toward an unruly tuft of red hair. 'Ashtar says you're to go straight to the training dome.' The kid motioned the board to depart.

Dharma halted him and threw the kit bag to the ground. She landed the eight-hundred foot jump with the grace of a house cat and stepped onto the back of the orb-board. Vega navigated the board with Dharma on the back, in and out of the giant trees and dangerous-looking shrubs until they hit a clearing, then seamlessly set towards an extraordinary looking dome.

'Thanks Vega,' she said, offering a high hand—he hit it back and shot towards the island's beach.

Dharma took a moment at the entrance of the Federation building, created from willing wood and graceful glass. A moment was apparently not time she had to spare, as an eager young clerk marched through the domed foyer, headlong towards her.

'Captain, you are to report immediately to the training dome,' the clerk barked, ready to escort her to the imminent briefing.

Dharma followed him to the entrance of the training dome and stalled under the entrance archway. The clerk ushered her to join the awaiting mission unit. Reluctantly, she stepped into the dome. The space stilled as Dharma quickly looked around at the rows of tiered seating, already filled with hundreds of agents, all looking in her direction. Her view was pulled to the radiating male figure holding centre stage. His glistening aura blended with his long golden hair, highlighting features that could only be described as majestic, with a hint of intergalactic.

'Dharma, please take a seat.' Ashtar said, his startling blue eyes, hypnotic pools of knowledge and knowing, gazing straight through her. 'Salva, welcome. Please pass into the Brodgar training dome.' Ashtar bowed and ushered the arriving agents to join the seated agents.

Dharma glanced back at the agent lingering in her shadow. Her eyes made an involuntary roll as she realised it was the man from the plane.

'It is my great honour to welcome you all to Brodgar.' Ashtar bowed and commenced the briefing. 'The Intergalactic Federation have summoned four hundred and forty-four elite agents.' He held out his hands as if acknowledging each one of those four hundred and forty-four intergalactic agents individually, then directed his hands skyward. 'And there you all are.'

The domed ceiling transformed into a holographic mirror of the multiverse. Silence circulated each of them, encapsulated and in awe of the interstellar view.

With the slightest motion of Ashtar's hand, the sky moved and the window to the multiverse zoomed toward a binary star system. 'Sirius!'

Ashtar's call was greeted with loud cheers, 'as always, loyal to the cause.'

The Commander set the night sky back in motion. 'Orion!' he boomed through the building wall of sound, and the ceiling spun into movement once more. A lull fell amongst the mission unit as the celestial-scape zoomed in on a single bright planet. 'Arcturus!'

Dharma uttered a cheer, only to realise her co-intergalactics were completely silent. She slid uncharacteristically down into her chair, quite apparently alone.

The night sky began to fade, and the ceiling painted by one of the greatest intergalactic artists of all time returned.

The story of the Brodgar training dome ceiling is legendary throughout the Federation. Michelangelo, it is told, arrived as a young cadet from Arcturus in the late 1400s, one of many arriving intergalactics at that time. Legend has it that Michelangelo refused point-blank to attend any scheduled training following his initial briefing at Brodgar, which he walked off from mid-briefing, announcing, *I have no time for any of this nonsense, I must paint!* He left the class, returned to the barracks, and began painting his small, domed quarters.

Commander Ashtar called for him to attend his chambers, but Michelangelo refused to stop painting. An agent was sent to the artist's dome. Stunned by what he saw, the agent rushed to Ashtar and tried to explain what Michelangelo had done, what he had painted. Ashtar immediately followed the agent. Upon seeing Michelangelo's dome, Ashtar arranged for him to receive all the supplies and equipment he required. The young artist painted much of the art at Brodgar, and when Michelangelo had completed his final works at the base, the training dome ceiling, he announced, *My training is complete. It is time to leave Brodgar.*

The artist served the Intergalactic Federation tirelessly, creating many great works throughout many of the Federation's bases. Yet it was his work within the Sarispa bases, as a covert agent, that created his fame on Earth.

'The Intergalactic Federation presents,' Ashtar announced as eleven holograms appeared in the training dome, 'The Council of Twelve.' The Commander introduced the governing peacekeepers of the multiverse.

All sound and movement ceased. Even in holographic form, it was such a rare sight to see, to be in the presence of The Council of Twelve; Dharma's body gave an involuntary shudder as she took in the vision before her.

'The Council of Twelve considered many ways to express to you the importance of this mission,' Ashtar said, addressing the collective. 'We have brought our presence here today as an expression of our commitment to you and all you may encounter. Each and every step you take, we, The Council of Twelve, will take with you.'

Dharma's gaze was drawn from Ashtar's golden glow to a female member of the Council. It wasn't the long blue sapphire cloak or the exquisite ancient jewel on her forehead, but that the lady's hologram appeared to be stuck in a time loop, the slightest repeating flinch of her hand, the same minuscule gesture over and over.

'Commander!' Dharma jumped to her feet, her shout was drowned by the piercing sounds of sirens ringing out throughout the subterranean island.

In a heartbeat, a reptilian claw reached out from the matrix and transformed its cellular shape, shifting to match its surroundings. The claw transformed into a humanoid hand and grasped for Lady Victorya.

A stun shot across the dome. Salva stood, hands raised, ready to stun again.

His warning shot had been enough. The humanoid hand retreated and the invading reptile sped back through the matrix. The dome filled with bright light, and the holograms of the Intergalactic Council faded, leaving behind the remnants of a rarely seen spectacular showing of optical phenomena.

'Thank you, Salva. Lady Victorya and the Federation owe you our deepest gratitude.' Ashtar, the only remaining member of the Council, bowed. 'I think it wisest that we continue the briefing at dawn.' The Commander's tone was mostly unwavering, yet the smallest hint of unease was audible.

The door to the training dome swung open. The stench of panic entered with a crowd of agents all heading towards the Commander.

Ashtar marched through the chaos and headed for his quarters. His calm was in direct contrast to his nervous following. He paused for a moment and spoke quickly and quietly to one of his charges. The agent turned and headed back into the training dome.

The hundreds of seated agents were now on the move. A burst of sound engulfed the entering messenger. The eager agent scanned the space, his task perhaps made a little easier by the flaming red of her hair, or possibly because she was the only agent still seated.

'Commander Ashtar requests your presence in his quarters immediately, Captain.'

Dharma acknowledged the messenger and continued to watch Salva walking through the dome, watching her.

How quick was he? She thought. *Very quick indeed.*

Chapter Three

Claw Gate

Despite the claw incident and being called to Commander Ashtar's quarters, Dharma was happy to be back on the island. A multitude of memories flooded her mind as she looked out to the ocean. So very far from home, yet this had felt as close to home as anywhere on Earth. Feeling like she could no longer delay going to see Ashtar, she headed into the constant stream of engaged agents congesting the route through the foyer and passageways towards the Commander's quarters.

Dharma presented herself under Ashtar's entrance energy scanner. The opulent archway lit and buzzed into action as the door unlocked and swung open.

'Take a seat, Captain, Commander Ashtar will be with you as soon as he's available.' A preoccupied female agent directed Dharma to a waiting area and sped back though the busy passageway.

Knowing that she could be in for a bit of a wait, Dharma made herself comfortable. Her instinct was correct—one hour passed and still no sign of the Commander. A fairly constant flow of Federation personnel, from commanders to cadets, kept Dharma mildly entertained; clearly 'Claw-gate' had created a bit of a stir. Fatigue filled her already heavy eyes. She closed them for only a moment when footsteps moved into her energy field. Through a partially open eye, she saw the swish of long, dark hair.

'Commander will see you now.'

With a heavy haul, Dharma picked up her bag and headed to Ashtar's office. A round table large enough to seat twelve sat centric, and Michelangelo's art breathed life into the Federation space. The once-still etchings, now animated expressions of interchangeable celestial scapes, acted as a window of insight into the entire multiverse.

Ashtar gestured for Dharma to take one of the remaining eleven seats. He finished signing documents for the awaiting huddle, and she scanned the celestial scapes, searching for real-time footage of home.

'Dharma, thank you for your patience. It has been quite a day so far. Can I offer you some refreshments?' Ashtar asked as the door to his chambers closed behind the last of his departing aides.

'No thank you, Sir,' she said, but thought, *a gallon of water and the biggest sub you got.*

'Sadly I'm all out of subs, but I am sure Leo and Nash will fix you something at their wonderful eatery.' Ashtar smiled warmly and poured her a glass of water.

Dharma returned an anxious smile. He, like she, was incredibly telepathic. Starting to feel uncharacteristic nerves through her hunger pangs, she hoped that this would be quick.

'Captain, it has been brought to my attention that earlier today and against direct orders you travelled to Brodgar via the matrix.'

'Sir, if I can have a moment to explain?'

'You may.'

'Commander Ashtar, I want you to know, it was a decision based on precise quantum calculations. It was brought to my attention that a dream-walker was present on the flight, an eight-hour flight from New Delhi to Scotland. Sir, I had just travelled cross-country for twenty-three hours straight without rest or sleep. If had I fallen asleep on the flight, I would have been an open treasure chest of information for the Sarispa.' Faintly feeling like she had it covered, Dharma sank back into her chair.

'Dharma, the Federation had it covered. We were aware the dream-walker was present on the flight.'

Dharma was confused. Why on earth would the Federation request she travel via terrestrial methods, then place a dream-walker onboard the flight?

'Always dynamic and brave, always willing to give all you have—excellent, in fact.' Ashtar spoke with genuine warmth, but he was unable to disguise the slight flush on his neck. 'Dharma, as a direct consequence of you failing to follow orders, a simple fixable glitch within the matrix has become a virtual wormhole.'

Dharma lowered her head, unable to look directly at the Commander. Not quite the start to the mission she had hoped for.

'No one was hurt, and the tech teams are working to shut down the wormhole.' Ashtar stood up, signalling the reprimand was coming to a close. 'Dharma, let this be a reminder, even our most dynamic agents still have areas to improve if they wish to reach their true potential. Trust, Captain, trust.'

Ashtar keyed a numerical sequence into a holographic screen; seconds later, the chamber flooded with dozens of eagerly awaiting Federation agents.

Mind numb and on the verge of exhaustion, all Dharma could think of was sleep. In a dream-like state, she began to navigate her way back through the Federation building. The much-needed air awakened her senses just enough to appreciate the views as she walked along the beach towards the barracks.

Random stuns and bursts of sand continued to land amongst a group of cadets trying to make the most of their break in the blissful surroundings. She spotted Vega playing Sphera with a group of Federation kids. It was a popular game amongst intergalactic children, originating from Orion. Short bursts of palm energy are moulded into the shape of a ball, and the 'buzz ball' is then directed at the other team. Hits above the waist lose your team ten points and stun the opposing firing player. Hits below the waist are the aim of the game and score your team eight points. Four players on each team, and multiple teams can play.

On the approach to the barracks an ocean-front café buzzed with life, and by the look of it, all incoming mission agents had hit it—all except Dharma, who wandered on by, really quite ready to hit the hay.

Two Pleiadean totem poles marked the start of the camp. She walked past what seemed like hundreds of small domed cabins to reach hers, which, she was happy to see, was as close to the water's edge as possible. The exhausted agent fell through the dorm door onto one of three low-lying futon beds. Instantly, sleep took her.

Flashes of dream-walkers and Lady Victorya flooded her sleep state, she followed the lady through a wormhole, fell, and landed as a child on her home planet. She watched the young Arcturian levitate stones, then send them skimming across the water. She caught a glimpse of an owl, and heard a high-pitched laugh. The laughter entered the cabin.

Dharma shot bolt upright, hands in the air, ready to act. Her vision was still blurred, but she made out two female Federation agents. She raised a gesturing hand and said, 'Hi.' It felt like an invisible weight had been placed on her. She lay back down involuntarily closing her eyes.

'Hello,' the agents said. One was short, with choppy chestnut hair, the other tall, with long, black satin hair; both were stifling laughter.

'Is that her?'

'Yes that's her. I escorted her to Ashtar's office this afternoon,' the tall, dark-haired agent said. One could only assume they presumed Dharma had gone straight back to sleep, their consideration of her was clearly audible. Dharma, now unable to get back to sleep and even more unable to ignore the loud rumbling of her stomach, sat up and lightly levitated to the edge of the bed, landing her feet firmly in front of them.

'Dharma,' she said, extending a hand to her new bunk buddies.

'Dorada.' With a slight squeak, the chestnut-haired agent gingerly shook Dharma's extended hand.

'Zeta.' The other agent stared intently at Dharma, and by the look in her murky green eyes, she was not impressed by Dharma's far-reaching reputation.

'Zeta, pleased to meet you. Dorada, it was a pleasure.' Dharma smiled at the agents, stepped away from the awkward exchange and headed out of the domed cabin, along the coved beach towards the oceanfront eatery.

Almost empty and pretty much closed for the day, it was perhaps the bright fairy lights that brought a twinkle to Dharma's pale blue eyes as she watched the two men dancing. Fully dramatized and perfectly coordinated, they wiped and cleaned the kitchen like the principle performers of a Mama Cass musical. The Laurel and Hardy silhouettes, clearly making their own kind of music, brought a stray and unexpected tear to the hungry intergalactic.

'Sorry petal, we're closed for the day,' Leo, a smallish, roundish man called without looking.

Nash, the taller moustached male, let out a frantic squeal when he saw who was standing by the café door. 'We really hoped you'd be back for the four-four-four detail.'

'But then we didn't see you this afternoon,' Leo said, grabbing her tightly.

'You need food, girl. You look actually starving.' Nash said, convinced she hadn't eaten a meal since they fed her last.

'I am pretty hungry.' She beamed at the duo.

Leo and Nash created an almost instant feast for Dharma. She sat on a stool at the counter and watched. The banter flew back and forth as quickly as the ingredients; at one point, pizza dough was vogued within an inch of its life. Satisfied that they had cooked up a small snack for her, they prepared a table at the water's edge and filled it with food enough for five.

'What happened, Dharms?' Leo asked, trying not to. Nash gave him a sharp look but he, too, waited for her response.

Dharma picked up a napkin, wiped her mouth and stared out along the shoreline. A single pebble began to levitate, hovering just above the others. She sent it skimming across the water. 'I don't know; I guess I messed up,' she said, picking out another pebble from the millions on the beach; she held it hovering just above the water, then released it. She watched the emerging ripples as if they might bring the answer. 'I don't know. I double-, triple-checked the matrix. I know command said it wasn't safe to travel, but when I looked I could see agents travelling, lots of agents. The full unit was travelling the matrix to Brodgar, so the passage looked safe.'

'Now girl, that's where we're lost, virtually the whole detail ...' Leo's voice trailed away.

'Nearly all mission agents arrived via the matrix.' Nash finished.

A couple of pebbles hovered; a multitude followed. Sensing a sonar ride, a colony of bats and a flying fox swooped in. Dharma released the stones and watched the show. Images emerged from the rippling pools of water lit by the moonlit sky.

'What do you see?' Nash asked, leaning in, attempting to view the vision from her angle.

'Oh, I've got it, see? Look over there.' Leo pointed to emerging watery apparitions of Ashtar and The Council of Twelve. 'Whatever the reason, lovey, Ashtar did not want you travelling the matrix today.'

'He really didn't,' she said staring out over the water, transfixed by the hovering puzzle pieces.

'But if you hadn't travelled via the matrix, you would've missed the briefing, I just don't get the logic. Not one bit.' Leo said, mimicking a reptilian claw.

'Stop it!' Nash playfully pushed Leo's hand away.

Ignoring their antics, Dharma began to gather herself, and the images over the water began to fade. 'For whatever reason, I wasn't meant to travel the matrix, but I did. It is what it is.' Appearing to let it go, she turned the conversation back to Leo and Nash and how fabulous they were.

The three old friends managed to fit in a few more stories before sleep chased Dharma. With the thought of a dawn briefing, she thanked and hugged her dear friends and headed back to camp. The dorm was silent and dark on approach, and for that, Dharma was truly grateful.

Chapter Four

The Four-Four-Four

Dawn arrived quickly. Zeta had already left for the training dome, Dorada was using the only bathroom in the cabin, and Dharma lay in bed remotely scanning the matrix. She looked for signs of unusual activity. Nothing was apparently visible. The glitch had been rectified and everything seemed as it should be.

'Are you heading up for the pre-briefing breakfast?' Dorada asked, the nervous squeak in her voice still a little audible.

'Don't think I'll make it,' she said, awakening from her remote view, 'but thanks, Dorada.'

Showered and almost awake, Dharma wandered along the shoreline picking out prime pebbles, considering yesterday's events. She aimed each skim at the random strips of floating land surrounding the island, an activity that took her to the training dome, exactly as she planned.

Habitually, Dharma took the same seat as yesterday and gazed up at the interconnected paintings on the domed ceiling. Aeons, Federation bases and leaders were all set into the background of the cosmos. She studied the portrait of Sophia, a great and primordial Aeon; as she did, a single purposeful light beamed out from the fresco, and forty-four Federation Commanders entered the dome.

'Welcome agents,' Ashtar broke the lull and set the early-morning briefing into action. 'For some, this may be your first Earth mission; for others, it will be one in a long timeline of missions. Regardless of our time previously spent on Earth or any other planet, you will now function as a unit, the four hundred and forty-four mission unit. Commander Castra, commanding officer of Brodgar C.I.T. will brief you on the updated training program.'

'Welcome to Brodgar.' A muscular Latin-looking man identified himself to the unit. The Sirian Commander carried an air of experience as he addressed the agents. 'Each of you will be put through a basic training programme in preparation for the upcoming mission; we hope and anticipate this will lead you to permanent Earth placements. Some of you will continue to remain within Counter Intergalactic Terrorism, others may move into other influential areas, such as global politics, ecological preservation, or perhaps you will become one of the progressive league of artists that cultivates expansion and growth.' Castra observed the newly formed unit. 'Standard Federation orientation training programs have been drastically decreased due to the pressing nature of the upcoming mission. We anticipate training will span over a two-week period. Should you reach the end of the assigned training period without fulfilling the required criteria, or unable to stay within a safe frequency spectrum, a replacement walk-in will be sought and you will be deployed to your home planet for reassignment.' Castra bowed, concluding the training update.

'Thank you Commander Castra,' Ashtar said and scanned the congregated officers.

'Commander Tara.' He introduced the Commanding officer of Stonehenge C.I.T.

An elegant, ethereal Arcturian agent moved through the sea of parting Federation leaders; her elongated stature and spiralling bright red hair stood a head above the intergalactic Commanders.

'Thank you, Commander Ashtar.' Tara's lyrical tones fell through a warm, open smile. 'You have elected and been selected from billions of intergalactic beings for your high skill set in your chosen field: Counter Intergalactic Terrorism. The Four-Four-Four mission has sat within Federation prophecy since the dawn of time. The sacred scriptures of the Great Aeons state the Four-Four-Four mission activates in the year 3033. Sadly, time has sped by, and Earth's doomsday clock is now calling the shots, sitting just one minute before midnight and a possible apocalyptic doomsday, with probable reverberating results throughout the multiverse. Earth and the multiverse are officially in a state of emergency.' Tara shared the message, bowed and stepped back into formation.

'Thank you Tara. An urgency does indeed surround the mission, if we have nothing further to add?' Ashtar asked, glancing around at the C.I.T. unit Commanders. 'Then let us assign agents and deploy all units to base.'

Through the hustle of agent assignment, Dharma sat tight. She had been a Federation Earth agent for thousands of years, and still, her intrigue and fascination for the processing reactions of new arrivals had yet to dwindle. Different planets vibrate at different frequencies, even within our own planet the frequencies will shift, hopefully, within a safe spectrum. We are able to adapt to a certain extent, but to move from one frequency to an entirely different one can be a challenge, even for active C.I.T. agents.

All agents arriving on a new planet are usually expected to spend a period of three days within a frequency chamber to align the intergalactic's frequency with the planet's frequency. For a number of reasons, some are just unable to make the required adjustments. Some will take a desk job within one of the Federation's bases, which gives them greater access to the frequency chambers, or, they return home.

Dharma watched the poorly, frequency-sick recruits recalling only too clearly the nauseous confusion and complete disorientation she felt upon arrival on Earth. Orientation can be tough; it can bring up all manner of systematic symptoms. In the early days, weeks and months, you feel like an out-of-tune radio. It's only the cadets who really want it, who truly want to serve and bring peace throughout the multiverse that succeed. C.I.T. is a calling, and not one that many hear.

The training dome gradually emptied, and the newly formed units deployed to their assigned Federation bases. Dharma didn't have far to go. She had been assigned to Commander Castra and the Brodgar unit, as she had hoped and anticipated.

Castra had held command at Brodgar C.I.T. for as long as Dharma could remember. Her awareness of him and his methodology was good. The Commander may have looked slightly out of place amongst the other Commanders; Castra still dressed like a rookie cadet. Dharma had long suspected this expression was to lull you into a false sense of security, because Castra was as break-neck as possible within intergalactic law, which is probably the reason Dharma had served with him for so long. Happy, and not surprised with her post, she set off to join her deploying unit.

Chapter Five

The Sarispa

Castra led the newly formed unit from the training dome to the C.I.T. base, a strangely quiet squad as they set off towards the north-west side of the hill. Dharma held back from the unit, watching the agent from the plane and Dorada support a frequency-challenged newbie making his way up the hill. Castra stopped walking and placed his hand on an unassuming indented rock. The hillside parted and revealed an ornate entrance. A scanner activated and the ancient stone doors slid into the hillside, revealing an entirely empty domed space.

Castra ushered the agents to gather in the doorway, and in the presence of the newly formed C.I.T. unit, the dome awakened. Overlapping spheres of light activated. Through the optical light show, a central command station emerged, then four stations to the left perimeter, and four to the right. The formation was complete, and Brodgar C.I.T. was ready for action.

'Come in and take any station for now,' Castra said, settling into central command.

Dharma, being an old hand, had her eye on the prize and headed to claim her station. Her movement awakened a flurry. The Arcturian took the station next to the dome's only other doorway, leading out to an encircling chamber-way and all other functioning spaces within the base. The entering intergalactics claimed a station, all except one—the young frequency-challenged newbie was still swaying in the doorway. The seated agents observed his Olympian effort as he staggered onto the dome's wall, hugging it until he reached the nearest station. An alarmed agent already occupying the space quickly removed herself as the struggling newbie raised his face, which now was foaming at the mouth, to offer a bubbly smile before he passed out.

'Would you both ...' Castra took control of the dome under the hill and directed Dharma and Phoenix, a young maverick-looking agent. 'Escort Rigel to the frequency chamber.' Castra scanned his wrist across the command station and brought up a live feed of the frequency chamber as he watched Dharma and Phoenix help Rigel onto an orbicular cocoon.

'Oh dear, Rigel's looking a bit green,' Castra said, activating the chamber.

Seven funnels sprouted from the frequency regulator. The organic tentacles searched for receptive energy centre; satisfied and strategically placed, the regulation commenced. Instantly, Rigel's body relaxed and the disorientation eased. Castra minimized the view of the chamber.

'As we are aware from the mission unit briefing, we are time-conscious, so we'll get straight to it.' Castra said, standing to brief the unit.

The domed ceiling zoomed in on the multiverse and stopped at the Draconian constellation. The formation of the stars illustrated the image of a dragon: proud, fierce and standing guard. The Commander zoomed the twilight scene into the dragon's eyes.

'Rastaban and Eltanin. Once home to a race known as the Sarispa. Both, technologically advanced planets; sadly, those advancements were not mirrored in their emotional intelligence. They blew each other out of existence. These are archive images, not a live feed. Thuban.' Castra said, manoeuvring the night sky towards the tip of the dragon's tail. 'Thuban is the Federation's elected Alpha Draconis and home to the only planet of dragons in the multiverse. Relations between the Federation and Thuban are peaceful for now. North celestial star to Earth until about five thousand years ago, the Federation has granted future North-star status in light of prevailing peace. The Federation has yet to create such an allegiance or alliance with the surviving reptilian races from Rastaban or Eltanin.' Castra paused for a moment, then asked the unit a question. 'What is the one thing that stops the remaining Sarispa from completely destroying each other?'

Half the group genuinely had no idea, completely in the dark; the other half were in the know, but as most of them didn't want to answer, it left only one.

'Young lady in the yellow?' Castra called to a nervous-looking agent.

'Earth ... Commander?'

'YES!' he shouted, 'What's your name?'

'Leda ... Sir.'

'Yes Leda, Earth. The colonization and control of Earth unites them. An ancient alliance brings them together, yet their only real allegiance is to themselves. Prior to the growth of the Intergalactic Federation as we now know it, those that could travel the matrix would travel the matrix. Some of the first intergalactics to successfully visit and conquer Earth were a group of Sauropsida from Rastaban and Eltanin.'

A still, cold feeling filled the dome, and for the newbie agents this was new intel. As Dharma glanced around the dome, her gaze stopped at Salva, who appeared distinctly sullen.

'The Sarispa's conquering domination of Earth is now of course intergalactic legend.' Castra continued, 'For over nearly two billion years, voyagers from Eltanin and Rastaban held rule on Earth. The original Sarispa, or as earthlings call them, the dinosaurs, were some of the first intergalactics to successfully travel the matrix and claim a planet. However, in a strange twist to their own reality, their reign of terror and domination was threatened. The entire multiverse was affected by the devastating destruction that took place within the Draconian constellation. The annihilation of Rastaban and Eltanin commenced the extinction of the dinosaurs. The last remaining bloodlines of the Sarispa dinosaurs were finally defeated by a highly advanced group of fire-breathing winged reptiles, the Thuban Dragons. Together with a league of giants, the rule of the Sarispa dinosaurs on Earth was brought to an end. Although,' Castra added, 'Sarispa organic matter helped to re-nourish and regenerate Earth, so, I guess you could say the DNA of dinosaurs or the Sarispa is the foundation on which life on Earth is based.'

The fresh intel brought an array of responses from the arriving intergalactics. Castra watched the dawning comprehension cascade over Leda's and Dorada's expressions. Zeta was a little too cool to let any emotion show, and sat unmoved by the intel. Rigel, the only other Earth newbie in the unit, would be brought up to speed when he balanced out.

'That's a brief look at the history of the Sarispa dinosaurs on Earth, and just out of interest, ternary readings show the Sarispa visited their time-removed relations on many occasions. OK, let's take a look at the hours before Rastaban and Eltanin annihilated each other.' Thirteen reptilian beings in their true Draconian form came into focus on the domed ceiling. 'Thirteen self-elected leaders stepped out of war,' Castra said, looking up at the ruling reptiles on the dome ceiling. 'A dark, devastating war gone beyond control or return, the thirteen leaders came together to form an Order. The Sarispa Thirteen. Six reptilian leaders from Eltanin, six from Rastaban, one with blended parentage. The Order, with its foreseen annihilation, looked interstellar; they saw Earth. A planet the Sarispa already held claim to, thirteen annual full moons, but perhaps most importantly at this point, at the point of their own planetary annihilation, were the Sarispa's active bases on Earth.' A light flashed on Castra's screen. He glanced at the station and continued, 'It was a direct repercussion to these choices that the Intergalactic Federation placed Counter Intergalactic Terrorism units on Earth.'

He paused. 'Good, OK. Rigel's grounded, let's take a break and resume in ten.' Castra signalled two male agents, Lupis, who was visibly older than the other agents, and a long-serving Sirian agent, Lynx.

The entrance to C.I.T. slid open, the dome filled with light and the thirteen reptilian leaders disappeared from the ceiling, while the agents headed outdoors to catch a breath. Castra asked Lynx and Lupis to retrieve Rigel, who was no longer experiencing convulsions, vomiting, disorientation or loss of consciousness but sitting upright and quite happy.

'Am I good to go?'

'You're close enough!' Lynx said, holding the door open for Rigel, who was still a little shaky, but with the help of Lynx and Lupis he made his way from the frequency chamber back into the dome.

'Take a seat Rigel, the boys will bring you up to speed.' Castra said, glancing up from his station.

Rigel sat down on the first seat he came to. Lynx and Lupis stood on either side of him and placed a hand on his head. Rigel froze, all except his eyes; even with his lids almost shut, the rapid eye movement was clear to see.

'And download complete. Take it easy, bud,' Lynx said, tapping the newbie on the back.

'I saw lizards, giant lizards; lots and lots of giant lizards ...' Rigel stammered and staggered to join the rest of the unit outside.

'Yes Rigel, lots of giant lizards.' Castra called after him, smiling, as the newbie navigated his way in Earth's Hollow Kingdom.

Chapter Six

Time Trials

'OK. Let's get you assigned to your mission units,' Castra announced and activated an orbicular command monitor. 'All Earth-based C.I.T. units operate with three unifying units,' he said looking at the newly assigned Brodgar agents. 'Terra Command: the unit working with the commanding officer. Terra-Alpha and Terra-Omega, two ground agents and two field agents within both Alpha and Omega. OK, let's get you hooked up. Agents assigned to Terra Command, Salva, Dorada and Lyra.'

The named agents looked to one another, not sure whether to be happy or not.

'Terra-Omega is Lupis, Lynx, Hercules and Zeta. Lupis and Lynx, unit field agents. Hercules and Zeta, ground control.'

Lynx and Lupis had worked together for as long as Dharma can remember, so no great surprise to her or them that they're back together for the four-four-four mission. Hercules, or Herc, as he preferred to be called, appeared to be delighted at the prospect of working with Lupis and Lynx. Zeta's reaction, on the other hand, was a little more reserved.

'Terra-Alpha agents, Dharma, Phoenix, Leda and Rigel. Dharma and Phoenix, out in the field, Rigel and Leda, bringing in ground control. If you're not sitting with your unit, please join them now.' Dorada and Zeta switched up and Castra continued. 'OK, let's get you logged in. Have you all got your Earth chip implant?' he asked, holding up his right arm.

An ID chip illuminated through his olive skin as he rotated around the dome, checking that each of the agents had been chipped. 'The chip allows you to log into your system here and all non-classified Federation Earth systems throughout the multiverse, with access to Federation buildings and the matrix. OK, scan your wrist over your workstation.' The dome lit as holographic screens and keyboards appeared on the agents' workstations. 'These systems may seem a little antiquated, especially if this is your first Earth mission. Sadly we're not able to run to our technological capacity on Earth; anyone know why?'

With zero offers of an answer, he randomly selected Salva. A little taken aback, Salva nervously cleared his throat and quickly repositioned himself in his chair.

'The advanced technologies of Arcturus or Orion, for example, would affect Earth's organic frequencies. The natural rhythmical frequency of a planet is likened to its heartbeat. Earth naturally wants to vibrate at 7.83 Hertz, yeah? Intergalactic technology increases electromagnetic surges, disturbing the planet's natural frequency. Our presence alone increases the planet's overall frequency.' Salva leaned in and lowered his voice. 'The Feds work with old tech underground mostly, in Earth's Hollow Kingdom, yeah? The Sarispa? Well, the Sarispa do what they do, and what they're doing is raising the roof of Earth. Not cool and they know it.' Salva stopped talking, sensing that intense silence you feel when you have shared a little too much.

'Thank you Salva, yes, exactly.'

Dharma watched him. His expression was neutral, but not the conversation in his mind. The entrance to C.I.T. illuminated and the shadow around Salva faded.

'Perfect timing!' Castra said, gazing at his screen.

'Fed techs, Pollux,' a stressed-looking ternary technician introduced himself, then pointed to the accompanying female agent. 'Mira. We're here to take the newbies through the systems?'

'Perfect, I'll leave you to it.' Castra said, standing. 'I'll take the field agents. They already have good working knowledge of the systems. Dharma, Phoenix, Lupis and Lynx, please.' Castra led the field agents out into the chamber-way, past numerous doorways, towards a solid titanium door. He waved his wrist over the security scanner. The doorway shot open, revealing the Ring of Brodgar.

'Bloody hell, it's Baltic. Come on chief, why do we need to work out here?' Lupis said, protesting through chattering teeth. The agents stifled their amusement at his tough-guy reaction to the Scottish weather.

'I'm really not laughing!' Lupis said, shooting them a dangerous glare.

'It's like the lad said,' Castra reasoned with the veteran agent, 'we have to work with old tech for the time being, and that means all agents—not just ground control, but field agents, too.'

'You're not actually serious! We can't run a mission on ancient travel methods. Come on, what are we talking here?'

'What we're talking is, well, we're talking leys.'

'We're talking leys, I flippen knew it! He's talking leys, guys, Castra's talking leys ...'

'I hear he's talking leys.' Lynx said, staring at the ground, shaking his head.

'It can't be done, Castra,' Lupis said, standing firm. 'Apart from anything else, no one has really travelled the ley lines for at least a hundred years. It's a rickety old roller-coaster, not fit for travel.'

'It's not that the Federation have put a complete ban on matrix travel,' Castra responded. 'I wouldn't allow that for a start, but look, it's a complex situation,' he said, looking at the agents, who all looked like they needed it really simple, really quick. 'Look … Dharma arrived via the matrix, an unauthorized journey, and it caused a parallel wormhole.'

'Thanks chief.'

'The Sarispa are watching the matrix for any and all glitches, anything at all. The Federation are attempting to shut down all matrix travel for the Sarispa, but it takes time and resources.'

'They're still able to travel, though!' Lupis quipped, 'the flippen Sarispa are still flippen travelling the matrix.'

'Our analysis shows simple results,' Castra said, holding his ground against their protests. 'The more general activity within the matrix, the easier it is for the Sarispa to penetrate our shields, track and trace us. As such, the Federation advises absolute minimal use of the matrix.' Castra called time on the discussion, but as a former field agent, he knew what he was asking his agents to do.

The matrix has become a highway for advanced intergalactic lifeforms, allowing almost instant travel anywhere on the planet, other planets, one timeline to another, almost instant travel from any one point to another. Matrix travellers hold infinite possibility; the Intergalactic Federation and the Sarispa both hold the possibility for transformation—the profound difference being? The Federation serves the multiverse, and the Sarispa serve the Sarispa.

'It's our heritage, how our ancient ancestors travelled around Earth,' Phoenix mused, gazing dewy-eyed at the stone circle. 'Come on, the ley lines are legend, man!'

'Legends belong in the past,' Lupis grumbled.

'Not all legends belong in the past, dude ...'

'Don't call me dude.' Lupis was clearly not amused or vaguely convinced.

'Who's up for it?' Phoenix asked, eagerly looking at the agents.

'Up for what?'

'Time trials? Buzz the leys!'

'Don't see why not. Buzz buddy for Phoenix?' Castra glanced between Dharma and Lynx, not bothering to look at Lupis. Before Dharma could offer an answer either way, Lynx jumped in.

'Go on then, where, to Giza and back?'

'Giza!' Lupis blurted, 'the Sarispa are all over Giza.'

'Exactly!'

'Let's keep it simple, keep it to a time trial not a war. Stonehenge and back?' Castra offered.

'Ya beauty!' Phoenix pulled in a punch and followed Lynx into the centre of the stone circle for a pre-buzz stretch-off.

'Idiots ...' Dharma said laughing, shaking her head at the agents exaggerated warm-ups.

'Positions, count down from three,' Castra shouted over the wind.

Lynx and Phoenix gave a thumbs-up, Castra called it, and the Ring of Brodgar stood empty.

'Phoenix buzzed the ley first and is just holding the lead.' Dharma commentated the race, following the action in her mind's eye. 'They're just about to hit the Loch Moy vortex.'

Unable to resist Lupis closed his eyes to watch the action.

'Is he? He did as well, Lynx jumped the ley at Loch Moy, he's heading down the Mavishow line. He's fast!' Dharma said, sounding impressed by the agent's pace on the leys.

'Lynx is on the return route!' Lupis suppressed a cheer.

'Roger that for Phoenix, it's close, too close!'

'Come on Lynx, come on lad… YES. Believe that's one-nil to Terra-Omega. Well done, lad!' Lupis called to Lynx as he appeared in the middle of the stone circle.

Less than half a second later, Phoenix landed. Lupis, a little smug at the Terra-Omega win, created a shiny ball from his palm energy and threw it to Lynx.

'Consolation ball? Nah, good buzz, bud!' Lynx said, passing the ball to Phoenix.

'The best!' Phoenix said catching the energy ball. 'Bring back the vintage tech, man. That's like going from flying an Arcturian craft to flying an old jet; I forgot how intense, how present it is.'

'I told you it's like riding a rickety old roller coaster. Anyway, when have you ever flown an Arcturian craft?'

'An agent can dream.' Phoenix replied, launching the buzz ball into the sea.

'Well done, agents. Lynx, the one thousand and eighty-eight mile round trip took you 10.5 seconds. Phoenix, 10.9. Close race, who's next?' Castra smiled at Dharma and Lupis.

'Unh-uh, not for me. I'm not riding the leys, Castra, end of story. It's not going to happen.' Lupis was set to walk away but turned back. 'I was one of the first Feds to work Earth and that's all we did, no matrix access none at all, zero, nada. I'm not, I'm just not doing it!' Clearly, Lupis was not, in any way whatsoever, going to buzz those leys.

'Dharma will win by default,' Castra said, holding back the slightest of smiles. 'If you're sure that's your final decision, will I call it? OK. Terra-Omega one and Terra-Alpha ...'

'STOP!'

'Yes, Lupis?'

'Just this once!' Lupis said, already walking to the centre of the stone circle, heading to quickly gain the prime spot to enter the vortex. 'It's a one-time event. Once only!' Lupis shouted to Castra who was looking on, fairly amused, as the agent took up his position.

'THREE-TWO-ONE BUZZ!' Castra called it. Dharma and Lupis vanished.

Lynx, Phoenix and Castra closed their eyes and followed the ley race.

'Dharma buzzed the ley first! Oh she's way ahead, no way he's going to catch her.' Phoenix called in with the commentary.

'He'll catch her, he's just getting warmed up.' Lynx said, defending his longstanding partner.

'She's almost reached Stonehenge,' Phoenix said, switching views to watch Lupis. 'He's slowing down, guys, Lupis is slowing down.'

'I see him, he's stopped at the Loch Moy vortex.' Lynx sounded worried. 'He's flipped, something's wrong. He's heading back up the ley.' The agents ran to Lupis as he emerged unconscious in the stone circle.

'What the hell happened?' Dharma shouted, arriving back at terra level seconds later.

'He needs a healer, Lynx give me a hand.' Castra said, lifting Lupis.

Chapter Seven

The Glass Pyramid

Deep below the Great Pyramid of Giza there is a pentagon-shaped chamber. Inside the chamber stands a hollow glass pyramid, and inside the pyramid is a three-legged stool. Bound to the stool, held captive to the pyramid, is an oracle, the Giza Oracle. A woman, a tortured, mutated soul whose wild expression reached for things that were not there, squealed in riddles and spoke in a dialect that was not of the Earth: she spoke the dark language of Draconias.

The Giza Oracle was watched. Her every rhyme and riddle was recorded by five Sarispa agents positioned around the glass pyramid, vigilantly monitoring the rapidly incoming intel.

Tirelessly, the agents watched and analysed the rambled reporting of the oracle and the incoming ternary code.

Few can truly read the ternary code in its full and disclosing form. Many can skim the surface of the code, decipher fleeting insights, events, actions and general activity, but for those who can truly read the ternaries, they hold within their sight an open view of the true history and secrets of the multiverse.

A Sarispa agent, positioned to follow the ternaries and the oracle, touched his ear piece and spoke into a mouthpiece. 'The Federation are active on the ley lines, Sir.'

'Coordinates?' A voice snapped back.

'Exact coordinates are not available, Commander, but an agent was detected at Loch Moy.'

'Did you detect the activity from the ternaries?'

'No Sir, the oracle picked it up.'

The entrance to the oracle chamber shot up, and a towering figure marched toward the agent. The humanoid form of the Commander could not fully disguise his true genetic make-up; his features, skin, hair and nails were mostly reminiscent of an Earth human, but once you know, all you can see is lizard.

‘Run the recording back,’ the Commander barked.

The agent brought up the recording of the woman in the glass pyramid. Her arms and hands moved in erratic, seemingly involuntary movements, and she searched for sight through her merged, mutated eyes. Fumes invaded the chamber. The oracle’s slumped body rose up, her imprisoned rhythmic motion heightened; she gasped in an inhalation of the noxious vapour and howled out a vision. *The wolf meets the obelisk at the heart of the pentagram, from the dark he could see, from the heart he did not run.*

‘You’re sure this is the only one?’

‘Yes Sir, no other detected recorded activity for the matrix or the ley lines.’

‘Lupis has his tail between his legs; Lynx cat will be upset. *From the dark he could see, from the heart he did not run.* How heartwarming.’

The Loch Moy obelisk tracker was activated over two hundred years ago, and this,’ the

Commander's eyes filled with action, 'is the first tracked activity.' An unnatural shadow grew around him. 'Pass my condolences on to his wife,' he laughed. 'How long has she been in there?' The agent fumbled for the answer. 'How long, Agent Messo?'

'Eight weeks, Commander Romorph.' The terrified agent answered like his life depended on it.

'Increase the dosage, double it.' Romorph said, watching the woman in the glass pyramid.

'The oracle is already at vape capacity, Sir.' The words left Messo's mouth, but as soon as they did he wished them back. The Commander's dark shadow closed in on Messo.

'Double the dose and—do—it—now.'

The glass pyramid filled with a noxious cocktail. The imprisoned oracle reacted to the rising vapour, a poisonous lifeline to the tortured, demented woman.

Romorph watched until he was satisfied she had received the next round of torture. His haunting shadow lingered long after he had left the oracle chamber.

Chapter Eight

The Yin to her Yang

Dharma and Phoenix headed back to the C.I.T. dome. The base was filled with chat and learning. Dharma pulled the tech teachers Pollux and Mira to one side. 'Would you have the agents run the Earth grid ternaries for the last twenty minutes? Orkney to Stonehenge, if anything jumps out,' she pointed to her head, 'message me, we'll be back in ten.'

'Where are you going?' Mira shouted after them.

See if we can speak to Lupis, he's down in the healing bay. Dharma said telepathically, attempting to keep the situation on the lowdown.

What's he in the healing bay for?

He hit a problem on the leys. Need those ternaries, Mira.

Mira briefed Pollux and gathered ground control agents. Sensing it was somehow mission on, they looked at each other, then at the empty seats of the absent agents before turning in trepidation to decipher the code.

Dharma and Phoenix walked down the hill towards the dome. Through the chamber-ways leading to the healing bay, they both experienced an unexpected flood of memories; the sight of Castra snapped them both back.

The Commander was talking to an elder healer in the healing bay reception. As she spoke and gestured, the silver stitching on the sleeves of her kaftan reflected a kaleidoscope of dancing rainbows around the serene space. Castra bowed and thanked the healer as she headed back into the healing bay to attend to Lupis.

'How's he doing?' Lynx asked, anxiously awaiting news of his Omega partner.

'Not great, by the sounds of it,' Castra said, pointing towards the seating area. 'They're not entirely sure what happened. The intel recorded on his chip is patchy. What they can see is, he intentionally slowed down on the approach to Loch Moy, tried to spin back before he reached the vortex, but the magnetic pull was too strong.'

'What did the vortex reading say?' Lynx asked.

'Tracking went down in the vortex; all they have is white noise for the time he's in there. The reading picks him up again after he exits. He's recorded travelling the return ley semi-conscious, arriving at terra level unconscious.' Castra reported, feeling visibly responsible for the accident.

'Can I use your station?' Dharma asked the agent who held reception for the healing bay.

He obliged.

She scanned her wrist and logged in to view her reading of the time trial. The agents joined her around the station. Dharma slowed down the vortex reading, it displayed nothing unusual: a building electromagnetic pull upon approach, heightened electromagnetics within the vortex, and a normal reading as she exited.

'Can we speak with Lupis?' she said, standing up from the station.

Castra approached the healing bay. Through a small circular porthole window, he could almost make out Lupis. The only light in the space came from an oculus in the ceiling and the healer. The circular cut-out cascaded, the healer glowed; both shrouded his writhing, unconscious being in a bright light.

Are we OK to come in for a couple of minutes, Ursa? Castra sent a telepathic message to the healer attending Lupis.

One by one, the agents entered the space, each of them pausing to be scanned—a dualistic scan that identifies the entering agent by their unique sound vibration. It also ensures the agent's vibration is within a healthy parameter, causing no further ill effect to the patient.

Each of the entering agents successfully made it into the healing bay, although, on approach to Lupis, denied access may have been preferable. He lay tortured. His head swung from side to side, his body writhed in involuntary spasms, he mouthed and motioned sound, but none was heard.

'You won't have long,' Ursa said, hovering a hand in the direction of Lupis's stomach. The writhing and random movement eased.

Castra and Dharma stood to the rear of Lupis and held a hand close to his head without coming into contact. The physical touch interrupts and lowers the vibration, making it more difficult to meet with the soul within the astral sanctuary. They attempted to connect with Lupis. Through well and healthy channels, astral communication flows with ease, but when the soul is lost without a map to the sanctuary, it can complicate matters.

Castra and Dharma stood in the stimulated sanctuary. It appeared as a clearing beside a river. They willed and waited for Lupis to arrive. Time was almost up; the healer wouldn't be able to hold Lupis' energy in alignment for much longer, and without the healer's aid, the agents had little chance of reaching the injured agent.

In the distance, a shadow appeared. Unable to walk or move, the apparition fell to the ground. Dharma set to move towards the phantom, but Castra stopped her. They watched the shadow of Lupis pull his hand through dirt and then disappear. Castra let go of her arm, and they sped to the spot where the spectre had appeared.

A message was etched out on the ground. The image was of a pyramid with an eye inside it; underneath the pyramid were two interlocking circles. The agents looked at the drawings, then at one another. In a wave of nausea and sadness, they left the astral sanctuary and returned to the healing bay.

The four agents bowed gratefully to the healer, then to Lupis, and exited the healing bay.

'What happened?' Lynx asked as soon as they had stepped out.

'Not here.' Castra said, marching through the building towards the main entrance, clear of the dome and any other agents. He stopped walking and looked at Lynx. 'The Sarispa have a Federation prisoner held at one of their pyramid bases.'

Dharma stared at him, dumbfounded by his filtering of what they both knew to be true.

'Is that all Lupis said, they have a prisoner at a pyramid base?' Lynx asked.

'He wasn't able to talk, he was barely able to appear. He fell to his knees as soon as he did. He managed to leave some markings on the ground, but that was it.' Castra said, looking out to the ocean, increasingly unable to look directly at Lynx.

'What were the markings on the ground?' Lynx asked, confused and chasing detail.

'A pyramid with an eye inside it,' Dharma quickly answered.

'That was it, nothing else?'

'Beneath the pyramid were two interlocking circles.'

'His wife ... the Sarispa have Rose? Is that what you're saying? Is that what you're telling me?' Lynx's expression told the horror each of them felt. 'It can't be, she's on a teaching assignment on Orion. She's been there six, maybe eight weeks, I saw her leave! She's teaching kids, man. Sick Sarispa scum!' Lynx slumped to ground.

'Don't worry bud, we'll get her back.' Phoenix held back his own emotion to console Lynx.

All the agents had known Rose for most of their lives. She had taught them all at one point or another.

'We'll bring her home, Lynx,' Dharma said, sitting down beside him, 'she's coming home.'

'He's not there, he's gone,' Lynx pointed to his head. 'Wherever she is, that's where he is, and he won't come back until she does.'

'We're bringing them both home.' Castra told him, still intently looking out over the ocean.

Chapter Nine

C.I.T. begins at Home

The entrance to C.I.T. illuminated. The ground agents looked up from the ternaries, distracted by the returning field agents and the timely apparition of Commander Ashtar. Castra and Ashtar shared a muted exchange then made their way through the chamber-way, towards the C.I.T. meeting room.

'Anything?' Dharma asked, pulling up a chair at the command station.

'Nothing yet.' Mira said, looking around the dome.

'Do they even know what they're looking for?' Lynx asked, slumping into a vacant seat.

'We have to give them time.' Mira said, studying the ternary code, her attention drawn back to the ground agents. 'Salva?'

'I think I might have something, watch this.' He played back a short portion of the ternary code, paused it, minimized the screen, then brought up a second screen. Their expressions were blank. 'OK, look.' He layered the two ternary readings. 'It comes out of sequence, there and there. This is Lupis at the Loch Moy vortex, and this is the Loch Moy obelisk. When you layer the code, the ternary fluctuation takes place at exactly the same time.'

'You're right, it does.' Pollux said, leaning in, spotting the tiniest of ternary glitches. 'Assessment of the echo?'

'The obelisk is a tracker, and it's picking up Lupis.'

Castra appeared in the doorway. 'Dharma, Phoenix, Lynx—if you've got a minute.' He gestured for the field agents to follow.

'Sir, Salva has something.' Mira said, stepping out of the growing conclave. Castra stepped in, as Salva highlighted the glitch and offered his hypothesis.

'It does look like the obelisk is a tracking device, albeit dormant until an hour ago.' Castra signalled for the field agents to follow him to the meeting room. 'Good work, Salva.'

Ashtar sat upright in a blue velvet chair, one of twelve positioned around the opulent orbicular table. 'Developments?' he asked, sensing the shift from the entering agents. Castra brought the Commander up to speed.

'Could we bring Salva in?' Ashtar requested, looking at Phoenix. Phoenix set off down chamber-way, reappearing moments later with Salva.

'Would you show me your findings?' Ashtar asked, gesturing for Salva to take a seat at the table.

Feeling momentarily perplexed, Salva froze.

Dharma pointed to her wrist.

The penny dropped as Salva activated a station and brought up the relevant portions of ternary code.

'Thank you Salvador, the picture is a little clearer.' Ashtar bowed and Salva rose to leave. 'Stay, the matter concerns you also.' Salva sat back down. 'We can confirm Rose left Earth fifty-five days ago, she travelled the matrix to Orion, arrived safe and well, however, we have no confirmed tracking following her arrival.' Ashtar's posture straightened in rigid alignment. 'The Federation are in the process of bringing a small group of Sarispa into custody on Orion and Earth. The Earth arrest awaits my command. I felt it better to inform C.I.T. prior to the event.'

'No way, the Sarispa in Brodgar?' Phoenix blurted, eyeballing each of them. 'No way!' He repeated. 'Here?' His stare stopped at Salva.'

'Tube, they're not going to be in here, are they?' Lynx said, shaking his head at Phoenix.

'Why not Lynx? They could be, they could be sitting in this very meeting room.' Phoenix's stare shifted between Salva and Ashtar, trying to gauge the Commander's response.

'Phoenix, they are not in this room.' Ashtar spoke quickly and lightly to Phoenix, holding back any heaviness.

'Sorry Commander, it's just, you know it's whoa ...'

'It is indeed, Phoenix,' Ashtar got up from his chair. 'Now that you hold this intel, your discretion is of the utmost importance. If I may, a private word Castra.'

Dharma headed back to the dome with Salva, leaving Lynx and Phoenix conversing in the chamber-way. Dharma stood at the entrance to the C.I.T dome; her distorted vision saw clearly. She knew it and ignored it, perhaps she was waiting. Either way, it was now confirmed the Sarispa had shape-shifted, brain-twisted, and tricked their way into a C.I.T. base—*her* C.I.T. base.

'Brodgar is on complete lockdown, no one can arrive or leave.' Ashtar informed Castra. 'All communication, telepathic or otherwise, has been blocked. I believe officers are en route to take the agent into custody.' Ashtar stood up, terminating the meeting. Lynx and Phoenix detected the Commander's movement and darted back to the dome.

Castra's monitor lit. Three officers stood awaiting entry on the other side of the door. He glanced at Ashtar, who nodded and sanctioned their entrance. Dharma watched the Sarispa agent, who try as she might could no longer conceal her increasing certainty that she was, indeed, busted.

'Zeta,' Ashtar called, addressing the Sarispa spy, 'all methods of transportation and communication are of course locked down. A full and total block is in place.'

The arresting officers surrounded Zeta. Dharma, Lynx and Phoenix instinctively took to their feet, palms poised.

Zeta's shape shifted. The pretty green of her eyes took their natural form, distinctly reptilian. Her skull elongated and her long hair regressed; her humanoid athletic form became rippled and pumped. Zeta knew she was cornered, and typical to the Sarispa character when backed into any corner, they will attack. Zeta displayed classic Sarispa traits. She would have covertly watched every action, recorded every fear and weakness. The Sarispa's will to take you down is their weakness.

'Ashtar ...' the humanoid reptile hissed out, 'we have you surrounded, the entire Federation cornered. Earth is in the palm of Sarispa hands, Ashtar, complete and total Sarispa domination.'

The arresting officers moved in closer around Zeta, poised, awaiting command.

'Ashtar, we control ninety-eight percent of the planet's money, banks, federal reserve—the entire financial structure is owned and controlled by the Sarispa. I think that means we own the planet, don't you? What about global political leaders? Well, how would you feel if I told you seventy-seven percent of the planet's political leaders are Sarispa leaders? Now I'm no mathematician, but I would say that's a majority. Two out of two, can you see where this is going? Earth's corporations, seventy-eight percent, media, seventy-three percent.' Zeta continued to spit out the Sarispa stats. 'You wouldn't bite the hand that feeds you, would you, Ashtar? Earth's farming and food manufacturing, seventy-nine percent and growing; now that is a tasty little morsel.'

The more Zeta spoke, the darker her growing shadow became. 'Ashtar, are you ready for this? Pharmaceuticals, what about Earth's pill-popping pharmaceutical industry? Fifty percent? Seventy percent? Nope, not even close. Ninety-eight percent. That's right, a nine and an eight, ninety-eight percent Sarispa owned and controlled. You've got to admit, Ashtar, we've got them and we've got them good.' Zeta stood for the cause, ready to die, prepared to impale her chip with a growing claw. 'I will die happy, Ashtar, Earth belongs to the Saris- ...'

A blinding light froze the Sarispa agent. Dharma had seen enough. She surrounded Zeta with an expanding sphere of enclosing energy. Zeta was locked down, unable to move, harm or self-harm. 'She might come in handy.'

'Indeed. Thank you, Dharma.' Ashtar turned to the officers. 'Please take Zeta to holding bay five.' The Federation guard escorted the Sarispa spy, confined by Dharma's stun, down the hillside to the holding bays.

The dome contracted and the agents sat in stunned, seismic silence.

Chapter Ten

The Serpent and the Tree

Prior to the formation of the Intergalactic Federation, galactic wars between Thuban, Rastaban and Eltanin were notorious throughout the multiverse. A constellation constantly at war, hell-bent upon destruction, death and planetary annihilation. Yet through the anarchy and complete annihilation of Rastaban and Eltanin, a revolutionary Order was born.

The Sarispa Thirteen forged. Through the dark shadows of war, a powerful binding alliance led by heinous Sarispa dictator, Lord Hitch, was created. One hundred and thirty-three thousand evolved intergalactic reptiles travelled to Earth. Through the journey, their natural reptilian form shifted, a normal occurrence for intergalactics that travel the matrix from one planet to another. The traveller adopts the inherent dominant physical form of the host planet. The one hundred and thirty-three thousand travelling reptiles were at the time the largest-ever collective of intergalactics to journey from one constellation to another, but not the first.

Hitch and the masters of the Order led the army of intergalactic invaders to an already developing kingdom. The Thirteen, in their acute foresight, had already dispatched an army of reptilian builders. Ten thousand highly skilled Draconian stonemasons arrived at Saqqara, Egypt and set to work creating some of Earth's first and oldest stone structures. They built a flat-roofed pyramid with thirteen doorways but only one entrance. A subterranean base and chamber-ways eventually connected the Saqqara base to their Giza base. The Sarispa underworld had begun.

Earth was not the only planet at the time to experience the wonders of the notorious reptilian builders. They built many bases upon many planets, perhaps in the expectation that somewhere in space and time they may wish to invade and conquer.

Without a planet to call home, the Thirteen and their following order of reptiles entered Earth. Initially residing at the Saqqara base, they stayed at the primordial Sarispa settlement just long enough to oversee the creation of the *Cobra Kings*.

Thirteen stonemasons skilfully carved thirteen cobras into the wall of a newly built sacrificial temple. Thirteen stonemasons served thirteen archetypal architects. To seal their karmic claim on Earth, Lord Hitch, master of the intergalactic order, held a ceremony. He summoned the dark and awakened the deep. A latent dark serpent that lay dormant within the land rose up.

In that moment in time and space, the gateway to Saqqara opened, the vortex vibrated, the plateau flooded, and a bright light delivered The Council of Twelve upon the Earth, poised and positioned to counter the Sarispa's claim, the karmic ownership of Earth.

Unable to remove the claim in its entirety, The Council transformed the dark, awakened serpent. A shadow that represented the embodiment of the Sarispa's ancestors on Earth transcended; a miraculous metamorphosis took place. The darkness that lay dormant within the earth was no longer dark, but a kaleidoscope of light and hope. A rainbow, a multi-coloured serpent now coiled around the core of the planet, was awakening and connecting vortices and intergalactic stargates.

In celebration and commemoration of the transcendental transformation within the planet, a seed sprouted and a tree grew, rooted in the underworld, reaching for the celestial sky, a bridge between both. A tree for all life on Earth.

With the voyagers' vagrant claim to the karmic ownership of the planet denied, the Sarispa divided their efforts to dominate. Lord Hitch led an army via the matrix to Mexico. Upon their arrival in Mesoamerica, the ancient aliens built many small, temporary settlements to allow for the passage of the equinox, ensuring precise celestial alignment with Orion and a perfect geopathic alignment with their developing subterranean Giza settlement. Terra-level pyramid structures and a Sphinx to guard the Sarispa's secrets would come later.

It was Teotihuacan in Mexico that was destined to become the first Sarispa city on Earth, a base for Lord Hitch to commence his planetary domination. The Sarispa built as they did on

Rastaban and Eltanin, underground cities with terra-level temples. The sacred geometry of the pyramid served the Sarispa well. How proudly they built their Mesoamerican metropolis, not afraid to show who they were. The first completed pyramid at Teotihuacan was lavishly embellished with statues of winged serpents, which forever held in stone their great flight to Earth. The Mesoamerican pyramid now known as The Pyramid of the Moon still to this day proudly stands on Earth. The millions of years since their first voyages, roaming the land as dinosaurs, had served the Sarispa well; they were now some of the most advanced beings in the multiverse. Yet, as evolved as they were, they still feared the dragons of Thuban.

The watchtower, the all-seeing eye in Egypt from where they would govern the sky, one eye upon Thuban and one upon Orion, gave clear sight to the dragons' direct routes to Earth. The celestial alignment in Mexico did not bring quite the optimum positioning they had first anticipated. Taking no chances, the Sarispa sought another.

The next Sarispa watchtower was not destined to be a pyramid complex with a subterranean base, nor would it take thousands of Sarispa builders or decades to build. A crevice within the Earth and a Pythia were the only requirements for the newly proposed interstellar observatory. An oracle was cast to play the unusual and quite often unwanted role of the Pythia. With the visionary help of the oracle, the perfect site was discovered. A group of participants followed the oracle through the matrix to Delphi. The small town in Greece held a rare and particularly powerful geological alignment. From a deep cranny in the ground, gases and vapours escaped from the Earth's grid matrix.

Seated upon the three-legged stool, the Pythia, the title bestowed upon the Oracle of Delphi, deciphered the intoxicating stream of vapour. Sensing and knowing any changes or variations within the matrix, the discovered knowledge was immediately communicated back to Lord Hitch and the Thirteen.

With a city and settlements en route, plus two watchtowers in place, the Sarispa held their most powerful position on Earth to date. The Federation governed the Sarispa as well as they could, limiting growth and colonization. The intergalactic reptiles quickly began to feel cornered and trapped. A growing anxiety and a lack of freedom led the Sarispa to take desperate measures, it led them to appease their great Maligno, the Quetzalcoatl, feathered serpent of the sky.

Human sacrifice became a daily occurrence at Teotihuacan, perhaps hoping the Quetzalcoatl would grant them freedom. Freedom to dominate and control, freedom to travel the matrix, freedom from the Federation, but really, there is no quicker way to have your alien activity shut down than to perform human sacrifice.

In light of these dark developments, the Federation dispatched a hundred and forty-four thousand agents to counter the Sarispa's growing attempted domination. The Federation's one hundred and forty-four thousand worked towards bringing peace and balance. Equally and always, the coin has a flip side. In this case, a Sarispa flip side, where control, manipulation and domination are far more equated to the Sarispa's natural disposition and inherent inclination.

Many of those hundred and forty-four thousand original Federation agents are still in service to this day. System reboot has become a familiar experience for the ancient intergalactics, Sarispa and Federation agents. When the physical form of the intergalactic dies, the spirit is carried quite automatically through the matrix to the point of creation, and a new life cycle begins. We are now dealing with a particularly dark and extremely experienced reboot of The Order of Thirteen.

Chapter Eleven

Download Complete

Ashtar departed the C.I.T. dome following discussions with Castra. The Commanders' conversations centred around the retrieval of kidnapped Federation agent Rose, being held at the subterranean Sarispa Giza base in Egypt. A standard trade was discussed: Zeta in return for Rose. Opposing intergalactics would meet within the matrix, and prisoners would be exchanged, in this case Zeta for Rose. That would be the Federation's objective; the natural objective of the Sarispa would be to take you down or take you prisoner. The wisdom of thousands of years lay deeply within Ashtar and Castra; the commanders were too wise to consider a trade.

Zeta was highly disposable to the Sarispa. A suicide bomber, she knew the risks of her mission. A trade was not an option. The Commanders concluded a rescue mission was required to bring Rose home, and with a couple of agents down they were going to need backup.

'OK, folks,' Castra engaged the unit. 'As some of you have not completed basic training, given the pressing nature of the arisen situation, time is no longer a luxury we have. Earth arrivals, we're gonna need you to download.'

The Federation often leads you to believe that a full training program will take place, but for an array of reasons, it very rarely happens.

'Terra-Alpha,' Castra said looking towards Dharma, Phoenix, Leda and Rigel. 'How you feeling, Rigel?'

'Good Sir, frequencies are balancing out.'

'Perfect, because you guys are up first. Dharma and Phoenix, escort Leda and Rigel to the download chamber.' Castra keyed in a numerical sequence, unlocked the entrance to the chamber and prepared the necessary downloads.

'Terra-Omega.' Castra swung around and looked at the two remaining agents in Omega,

Lynx and Herc. 'Herc, I'm gonna pull you out of Terra-Omega and bring you over to Terra-Command. Salva, I'm assigning you to Terra-Omega field with Lynx. Agents to cover Omega ground are en route.' Castra's screen lit. 'And they might need a download or two.'

'Sandwich, anyone?' Leo and Nash chimed in the entrance, shimmering in the doorway, laden with baskets of food and drinks.

'For those of you who don't know,' Castra introduced the double act, 'Leo and Nash, they're walking in as replacement ground agents for Omega.'

'We thought nothing would get us out of retirement, but when we heard about Rose and Lupis,' Leo's voice dipped.

'It was a no-brainer.' Nash finished.

'Eat! You all look starving.'

'Wow, are you guys standing in for Lupis and Zeta? Well, you know, not standing in for Zeta,' Dharma said, arriving back in the dome with Phoenix.

'We sure are, kid. Back in business, baby. You both look super starving, sandwich?'

'Hank Marvin, don't mind if I do.' Phoenix said, grabbing a sandwich.

'How are the downloads going?' Castra checked in with Dharma.

'Good, they're racing through them. We left them on quantum mechanics on Earth with an anticipated remaining download time of eight minutes.'

'Perfect. OK guys, this is how we're going to roll out the units. Terra-Omega, Leo and Nash on ground control, Lynx and Salva out in the field,' Castra announced. He was instantly faced with Dharma who, upon hearing the Omega field agent assignments, marched straight to his station.

'With all due respect, Commander, is Salva a field agent? I have never encountered him out in the field, not once.'

'Dharma, you cannot portend or assume you know all one hundred and forty-four thousand Federation agents, and as you know, many opt to reboot in a different physical form.'

'No Sir, I do not, but I know a Federation agent when I feel one,' she replied. Her whisper was low but her stance was strong.

Salva sat silently awkward, not fully able to make out the exchange, but he knew it involved him.

'Perhaps all our senses are heightened after our experience with Zeta this morning.' Castra said, looking towards Salva, attempting to defuse the awkward exchange.

'Maybe,' she said, letting it slide for the time being.

There was a block around Salva, and for one reason or another she couldn't see his timeline; it was completely blocked from her view. She might not have been able to see, but she could feel, and what she felt made her feel uncomfortable. But really, she had no desire to make any further cracks in the team, not at this point, not when it was about Rose.

'Wow, you've got to try that, have you tried that?' Rigel called, swaying back into the dome with Leda, who also appeared a little disoriented.

'Take a seat, guys. It can bring on a real light-headed feeling when you download so rapidly, you'll be fine in ten.' Phoenix said, guiding the spaced newbie Earth agents back to their workstations.

'OK, Leo and Nash you're up, let's get you downloaded.' Castra gave the veteran agents the nod.

'Want one?' Phoenix asked grabbing another sandwich. Dharma shook her head and followed Leo and Nash to the download chamber. They hooked up the downloads and headed back to the dome. 'What's your problem with Salva then?' Phoenix asked on the way back.

'I'm not sure that even I know. I can't see. I look for his timeline and I don't see it, I don't see anything, what do you see?'

'It's blocked for me too, but I don't see the way you do, Dharma, maybe you're not meant to see?'

'Maybe you're right,' she said, sitting down at her station, 'maybe Phoenix, just maybe, you're right.'

Chapter Twelve

Ley Line Route

'OK designated route to Giza.' Castra announced, and a map of the global ley line systems filled the agents' screens. 'Field agents, from Brodgar buzz north to Shetland, through the Stanydale Temple vortex, then take the southeastern ley to the Delphi vortex. From Delphi, take the direct ley to the Giza pyramid vortex.' Castra glanced around at the agents. 'I'm sure most of you have worked it out; field agents, we're asking you to travel through the Nazi pentagram.' A grimace fell over the field agents, and a distinct shift reverberated around the dome. 'Ground control, watch out for frequency fluctuations as your field agent travels through the pentagram.'

There was not an experienced Earth agent in the dome, field or ground that didn't roll their eyes at the route choice. Those that buzz the pentagram ley system have no doubt of their location; it feels like no other place anywhere on the planet. The Sarispa Thirteen that rebooted as Adolph Hitler experienced many incarnations on Earth, and that particular reboot was especially dark. The legacy of the darkness is etched within the Earth's grid.

'We'll be fully shielded, right?' Phoenix asked, perhaps recalling past journeys.

'You'll be fully shielded,' Castra said, reassuring the field agents. 'But,' he added, 'even with full and functioning shields, we can't completely guarantee that the prime resonance frequency you'll be travelling through won't be felt. Your every motion on the leys will be monitored; ground control will manually adjust the frequency within your shields, so, fingers crossed, you should stay within harmonic resonance. If you do hit turbulence, be still, have faith and know ground control have got you.'

'We got you, ladies,' Leo chimed.

'Once you reach the outer radius,' Castra said, briefly glancing at Leo, skilfully disguising his passing amusement, 'ten kilometres out from any of the manned vortices, ground control will place a sonic block around you. The blocks should allow you to pass through the vortices undetected. OK. The Giza vortex is active directly underneath the Great Pyramid, directly above the entrance to the sub base. When you exit the Giza vortex, follow the western chamber-way. We believe Rose is being held in an oracle chamber within the sub base. Herc, send the coordinates to the field agents' chips, for natural navigation.'

'En route.'

'Coordinates for the return journey?'

'Incoming.'

'We presume Rose will require specialist healing. It's also highly likely the Sarispa will have implanted a tracker. The Federation have arranged for her to be received at the Grange Healing base in Limerick, Ireland. Rose's tracker will disable on the Irish leys. OK: return route, from Giza, buzz to the St. Peter's obelisk vortex in Rome, from Rome to the Bosnian pyramid vortex.'

'Sir?' Lynx interrupted, confused, confounded even, by the Federation's choice of return route. 'Aren't the Rome and Bosnian vortices active, heavily manned bases?'

'The last place the Sarispa will anticipate you heading is straight through their manned vortices; ground control will have you covered with sonic blocks.' Castra said, glancing at Lynx, who just about managed to feign a look of confidence. 'So from Giza to Rome, Rome to Bosnia, through the Bosnian vortex to the Grange healing base. Good, OK, look, you'll be on Sarispa soil, we know of at least one oracle at the base, an oracle that knows each of you, which means it's more likely she'll detect and alert the Sarispa of your arrival. Rose will be under a noxious chemical influence, so her heart will connect to you and her head will detect you far more easily than any Sarispa oracle could. Questions?'

'Do we know how many Sarispa agents are stationed at the Giza base?'

'The latest ternaries show six agents in close vicinity to Rose, I would assume a greater undetected number throughout the base, any other questions?'

Nervous tension filled the dome, mostly from ground control, the field agents switched the necessary switch and were ready to deploy. Castra gathered the energy of the entire unit, each of the intergalactics stood, individual streams of light become a collective.

'Do this!' Lynx let go.

Standing in the Ring of Brodgar ready to buzz the leys, the field agents heard a whisper in the wind. Lupis had summoned the will to momentarily, energetically, join the unit as they headed out to rescue his wife.

'Who's mission, Alpha?' Phoenix called to Castra, realising that they might need more than the memory of Lupis to lead the unit.

'Dharma,' he called back, watching the field agents prepare, and then disappear from the stone circle.

'Game on, agents have buzzed the leys.' Herc updated Castra as he re-entered C.I.T.

'Remember: the more meticulously you follow the ternaries, the safer our agents will be.' Castra called, taking position at the central station. He glanced around the dome. From their concentrated expressions, the magnitude of the journey was becoming a reality to the ground agents.

'The Shetland vortex stats are in.'

'Agents are on the approach to the Nazi pentagram; prepare to manually adjust harmonic shields.' Herc called, alerting the unit to the potential upcoming turbulence.

'Let's rock and roll, ladies!' Leo cheered as if retirement had been a dull dream.

'Manually readjust harmonic shields.' Castra called, the unit synchronistically protected the agents travelling through the Nazi pentagram.

'Dharma and Phoenix are experiencing minor vibrational turbulence,' Leda reported, holding back any audible panic.

'Copy that.'

'Harmonics are holding for Lynx; Salva not so much.' Gone was the rock-and-roll from Leo's voice. 'Salva's going into a spin, Castra?'

'It's never gonna be a comfortable buzz through the pentagram,' Castra quickly brought up Salva's ternary reading. 'Leo, raise his shield. Raise Salva's harmonic shield!'

'We're raising his shield; it's sending him into a spin.'

'Lower it an eighth of an octave.' Herc said, calmly instructing the duo.

'What?'

'Lower Salva's shield an eighth of an octave.'

'Just do it now, before you lose him,' Castra shouted at Leo, ready to pass the task to Herc, not about to let his agent go down on the leys.

'Got it, thanks Herc. Sorry, Salva.' Leo said, apologising to Salva's stabilising code.

'Is he good?'

'He's good, Castra. Owe you one, Herc.'

'You'll owe me more than one by the end of this.'

'Cheeky monkey.'

'C.I.T., focus. Agents are approaching the outer radius of the Delphi vortex. Remember, this is an active base; the Sarispa are still in full use of the vortex.' Castra brought the unit's attention back to the approaching heavily manned vortices, and he guided ground control through the pending protocol. 'Hold standard shields on approach; when your agent reaches the ten-kilometre outer radius, activate the sonic blocks, then again when they reach the ten-kilometre outer radius, take the shields back to a standard harmonic alignment.'

'Agents are on the approach, twenty kilometres out from the Delphi vortex,' Herc called to the unit. 'Dharma is leading on the ley, Salva, Lynx then Phoenix.'

'Prepare sonic blocks, fifteen kilometres; hold it,' Castra said, taking to his feet. 'SONIC SHIELDS.'

'Salva's safe and sound with a sonic shield.' Leo called, awakening a round of responses.

'Dharma's shielded.'

'Lynx is shielded.'

'Phoenix, too.'

'All agents have successfully passed undetected through the Delphi vortex.' Castra said, preparing the ground agents to lift the sonic blocks. Prolonged ley travel with a heightened harmonic can cause the agents issues, and issues for the leys themselves. 'LIFT. OK, folks, this is it, we're on. Agents are on approach to the Giza vortex.'

The ground agents meticulously followed the incoming code. Castra whispered under his breath. His lips moved, but his sound was silent, holding command until the precise, exact moment prior to the agents reaching the outer radius of the Giza vortex.

'ACTIVATE SONIC SHIELDS.' His sound was no longer silent. 'Field agents have successfully landed; repeat, agents have landed, deactivate travel shields.' Castra called it through a collective brief exhale of nervous energy.

The agents continued to follow the field agents' code as they entered the Sarispa's Giza pyramid base.

Chapter Thirteen

Operation Rose

The vibrant amber hue streaming from the sphere of planetary energy dulled. The Brodgar field agents stepped out of the Giza vortex and headed down a steep declining chamber-way. The air thinned and became musty-tasting. Dharma held up a hand, halting the unit as they approached the entrance to the ancient Sarispa base. She scanned the downloaded coordinates and silently signalled to the agents; once out of the chamber-way, they would head north through the great hall to the midsection of the base; the entrance to the oracle chamber was situated between archway six and seven.

The agents stepped out of the chamber-way into the vast subterranean space. Dharma caught Salva's mesmerized expression. His gaze followed the line of thirteen imposing, impressive archways spanning the length of the magnificent hall. Thirteen unique archways and supporting pillars, representing the thirteen masters of the reptilian Order. Coded into the stone pillars, hidden in clear sight, their quests, roles and heritage; even the Thirteen's unique harmonic resonance was covertly engraved into the overtly ornate stone pillars.

It's a ghost town, Dharma thought, checking the space before heading out. It was hard to believe that the deserted base had once been a thriving Sarispa settlement, holding global command and control. *Now,* she thought, *they just kidnap old ladies.*

'A drone.' Salva whispered, spotting an armed mechanical spy.

'Where?' Dharma's vision darted throughout the haunting space.

'Just zipped behind the third archway, left pillar.'

'Got it.' She whispered, shutting down the pentagon-shaped drone. 'Pillar to pillar, and don't tell me you've seen a drone just shut it down.' She signalled for the unit to move out.

They left the cover of the primal pillar, an entirely elaborate piece of masonry, yet still the most basic of the thirteen monuments in the great hall, which only increased in magnificence towards Hitch's apotheosis at the northern end of the base. Running in swift, tight formation, the four sped to the next archway.

Dharma edged just beyond the second pillar. At first glance, the hall appeared to be void of any visible Sarispa guard. She readied to give the signal when a moving shadow caught her line of vision. The agents simultaneously surged up an embellished column, giving them a clear visual of the incoming swarm of drones. They aimed and fired. Multiple flashes of light silently shot across the grand Giza hall.

'Drones are only stunned; we haven't got long.' Dharma whispered, preparing to leap down.

Salva grabbed her arm. She eyeballed him and then saw it. An eerie form, the head of an eagle on an elongated humanoid body, with the wings of a Nephilim. The Anunnaki guard floated past the unit and disappeared through a ceremonial doorway beyond archway thirteen.

The unit reached the sixth pillar. Dharma pointed beyond the pentagram-embellished column towards a black metallic door, situated between archways six and seven. She gave the command, and the agents sprinted towards the oracle chamber. Dharma shot a stun at the entrance, but the door didn't budge. She tried again with more voracity; the stun bounced.

'Maybe …?' Salva said, aiming his palm directly at the security scanner. The entrance to the oracle chamber shot open.

Four out of the five Sarispa agents failed to look towards the opening entrance. Their attention vigilantly remained on their screens, presumably assuming it was base Commander Romorph entering the chamber. The one agent that did look up froze. Faced with the Federation four, his stunned expression told the story of his real-time terror. Four simultaneous flashes followed, debilitating the remaining all-seeing eye unit.

'Clear. Shut down the vape.' Dharma called, holding her palms towards the glass pyramid.

'Vapes are shut down, chief.' Phoenix said, stopping the flow of gases to Rose.

Dharma's hands lit, and a flame of crimson light commenced its rise. She directed the growing phenomenon towards the pyramid; the glass shook and returned to sand.

Lynx and Phoenix ran to Rose. Lynx lifted her frail frame into the cradle of his arms and drew her close, resting her mutilated face on his heavy heart.

'You OK?' Salva asked, watching the ruddy wave of energy subside around Dharma.

'I'm fine, let's get out of here,' she said, turning towards the exit in time to see the metallic door open.

Stuns left Dharma's palms before the door was fully open, and Commander Romorph hit the ground.

'Take cover,' Dharma called, stepping over Romorph's crumpled body. She ran, flipped midair and hovered just below archway number six. 'Drones are starting to stir.'

The awakening drones sent befuddled shots towards her elevated position. A shield grew beyond her, buffering the incoming fire, sending the attack back to sender and shutting down the bewildered pentagon spies. 'Move out.'

Salva joined her, and from their elevated position they covered Lynx and Phoenix as they ran through the base, carrying Rose towards the entrance to the chamber-way.

'The Anunnaki guard is due back any minute,' Salva warned, sensing the approaching presence of the winged watch.

Dharma and Salva raced at an unearthly speed through the great hall. Salva approached the entrance to the chamber-way and Dharma slowed her pace. Sensing a presence, she stalled.

A dark sphere of energy engulfed her, immobilised, temporarily paralysed, imprisoned by a haunting black pentagram.

'Move out,' Lynx shouted. The agents in the chamber-way froze. 'Move out,' he shouted again, ordering the unit to continue on to the vortex.

'You can't just leave her there!' Salva shot back, bewildered, looking between Dharma's debilitated body and Romorph's approaching presence.

'If we stay, we all get captured. Dharma can look after herself. Move out,' Lynx shouted.

With Romorph enraged and on their tail, Lynx continued on with Rose toward the vortex. Salva looked at Dharma. As immobilised as she was, she had a look in her eye that said, *Get the hell out of here!*

No longer overwhelmed with indecision, Salva shot through the chamber-way, catching the rest of the unit as they approached the vortex.

The agents looked back, although they knew they wouldn't see Dharma. They entered the vortex without her and disappeared from the vibrating sphere of planetary energy.

Chapter Fourteen

When in Rome

'Agents have entered the Giza vortex; repeat, agents have entered the vortex,' Herc called, updating the ground agents.

'That's not right, something's up.' He murmured, still scrutinising the code. 'Correction, three agents and an unidentified traveller.'

'Rose will read as unidentified. Her Fed chip was discovered on Orion,' Castra said, closely watching the incoming code. 'Dharma, where the hell are you? Anyone picking her up?'

The dome remained silent. 'Run a deep trace on her, Herc. Son of a ...' Castra banged his fist on the desk, sending cups and papers flying across the dome.

'Soup sandwich?' Leo gingerly offered.

'It's a soup sandwich, all right. Anything Herc?'

'Yip, got her, and by the looks of it I'd say she's just about to break free of a Sarispa stun.'

'Who locked her down?'

'Romorph,' Herc squinted.

'Whoa, that girl can pick her fights!' Leo said, rolling his eyes.

'Ground control, continue to follow your field agents buzzing the leys.'

'You've got to get her, Castra,' Leo pleaded. 'You can't just leave her there, they'll kill her or worse!'

'Return to the ternaries Leo, agents' lives are at risk. Terra Command, all eyes on Dharma.'

'Copy that.'

'Agents are approaching the Rome vortex, Sir,' Leda called out.

'Turbulence?'

'Stable at the moment, Sir.'

'How's she doing, Herc?'

'She's holding her own, but it looks like ... yip, she's got company on the way.' Herc spotted the incoming swarm of drones.

'What the hell is she up to?'

'She's on the move, man, watch the speed on that!' Herc said, following Dharma's ternaries.

'Field agents and Rose have successfully passed through the Rome vortex and are en route to the Bosnian pyramid vortex,' Leo announced in a posher-than-usual voice.

Brief, nervous laughter filled the C.I.T. dome.

'Agents, focus!' Castra was not amused. He squinted at his monitor. 'Herc, is she running along the ceiling?'

'She sure is, never seen an actual ceiling run done at that speed before.' Herc sounded impressed as he commentated the unfolding action. 'Drones are on her, at least seven of them, two more and another, nine drones approaching. She's running towards them, she's … drones are stunned, she's on the move again.' Herc called, rapidly scanning numerous screens of code. 'We've lost her, no incoming ternaries.'

'Double-check. Terra Command, anyone got her?'

'Mission Rose is approaching the Bosnian vortex,' Leda updated the unit, 'incoming electromagnetic waves, preparing vibrational shields.'

'Copy that.'

A prolonged silence ensued throughout Terra Command. Streams of code filled their screens, but nothing to indicate the presence of a C.I.T. agent anywhere within the radius of the Giza Sarispa base.

'Dorada, open up the coordinates.'

'Yes Sir, three kilometres and growing.'

'Anything?'

'Nothing yet, Sir. Five kilometres.'

'Keep going ...'

'Mission Rose has successfully passed through the Bosnian vortex, agents are en route to Ireland,' Leo updated, briefly glancing at Castra.

The strain of an agent lost in action was starting to show on the Commander's face.

'What the ... shut the ...' Herc stammered, triple-checking the incoming code.

'Herc?' Castra quizzed, then he caught it. 'What is that?' he said, watching streams of incoming intel flood his screen.

'WHAT?' Leo and Nash screamed simultaneously.

'She's alive.' Castra called back. 'How the hell did she get that?'

'WHAT?'

'Dharma's fine. Leo, follow the ternaries. How the hell did she get that?' Castra said, looking at the screen in astonishment. The Commander watched classified Sarispa files download onto the Federation system. 'Lock up the treasure, Herc, block any trace. Lyra, contact Pollux and Mira, inform them we have incoming top-secret Sarispa intel.'

'Dharma's back online; repeat, Dharma's online!'

'Gonna actually kill her when I see her!' Leo said, looking more relieved than he sounded.

'Operation Rose is on approach to the Grange vortex, no predicted turbulence.' Rigel reported, relieved that at least one of his Alpha field agents was approaching the designated destination.

'Copy that.'

'We've lost Dharma again,' Herc said, frantically searching for a track or trace of her.

'I've got her, she's on the matrix,' Leda said, sending out a link of Dharma's active coordinates.

'Dharma is active on the matrix?' Commander Ashtar appeared on Castra's screen.

'Yes, we've just received the intel.'

'She's got company,' Herc interrupted the Commanders, 'two Sarispa agents have just entered the matrix after her, she's preparing to exit.'

'Where?' Castra shot back, although he already knew the answer.

'Vatican City, Rome. Looks like she's heading towards the Vatican vortex.'

'St. Peter's Square obelisk, interesting choice, Dharma. Keep me updated, Castra.' Ashtar graciously bowed out and disappeared from Castra's monitor.

'The field agents and Rose have successfully arrived at the Grange healing base.' Rigel called out to the dome.

'Good job, well done everyone.' Castra offered a heartfelt yet distracted thanks to the ground control agents.

'Sir …' Herc tentatively alerted the Commander, 'Dharma has entered into combat.'

'In the middle of St. Peter's Square?' Castra shot back.

'Yip, hand-to-hand combat, no signs of energy combat showing yet.'

'Flippin fantastic! She's doing Kung Fu in the middle of St. Peter's Square! Hold on, Dharma, we'll fly in a neon sign for you, or better still, let's just hover a craft into Vatican City and pick you up!' A female agent appeared on his monitor, and his mood momentarily shifted.

'Commander Castra,' a soothing lilt sounded out from his station. 'Your detail has arrived one short, but I am sure you already know that. Your three C.I.T. agents are well and good, and we have a team of healers working on Rose as we speak. We'll bring you further updates as we get them.'

'Thank you, Chiron.' Castra said, smiling back at the beautiful ethereal vision on his screen. The Commander appeared decidedly more peaceful than moments before. Chiron smiled back, bowed, and vanished from Castra's screen.

'Herc, how's she doing?' The entire unit had crowded around Herc's station to watch Dharma's Vatican action play out.

'Kicking ass!' Leo squealed, clinging tightly to Nash. 'One down, one to go!'

'Swiss Guard are heading in her direction. One, two … make that four Swiss Guards en route; they're firing arms, Sir.'

'Get the hell out of there, Dharma!' Castra screamed at the screen.

It was as if she heard his command. Dharma sped towards the Vatican obelisk and disappeared from St. Peter's Square.

'Swiss Guard have taken down the remaining active Sarispa agent.' Herc reported, continuing to commentate the unfolding action. 'Dharma has buzzed the leys and is en route towards the Bosnian vortex.'

'Copy that.'

'Sir!' Herc attempted to gain Castra's attention through the growing relief. 'The Sarispa files have been downloaded and deciphered. Sir ... you're gonna wanna read this.'

Chapter Fifteen

The Lyrical Light of Limerick

A sunken stone circle illuminated. Rays of green rose from the circle's henge, activating multiple interconnecting spheres, announcing an imminent arrival. Phoenix, Lynx and Salva rested up, sitting just beyond the ancient glowing earthwork, taking in the blissful views, and Dharma's arrival.

'Took yer time ...' Phoenix shouted, as her holographic form became a physical reality in the Lough Gur stone circle.

'Had a bit of business. How's Rose?' Dharma asked, climbing the henge to join them.

'Not great, but she's got a team of healers in with her,' a wave of nausea revisited Phoenix as he recalled Rose's condition. 'What happened to you?'

'Romorph hit me with an energy lock.'

'I know Romorph hit you with an energy lock, what happened after that?' Phoenix asked, watching a smile spread over Dharma's face.

'Seemed a bit nuts to bust into the all-seeing eye and not see anything.'

'Eh ...?'

Phoenix's confusion and Dharma's resting were both interrupted by the apparition of healing base Commander, Chiron. 'Dharma, are you well, my love?' The elegant healer gathered her flowing silver tunic and sat down beside them. Dharma pulled herself up onto her elbows. 'As you were, Captain. Castra can wait a little longer.'

Dharma smiled at the healer. Chiron's presence coupled with the charming geology brought Dharma a much needed and familiar recharge. The Grange was one of the first Federation Healing bases built on Earth. The Sarispa had already begun the tremendous task of building the Egyptian and Mexican settlements; both were not yet complete when the

Federation hastened to counter their presence on Earth.

The remote Scottish island of Orkney was selected to host one of the very first C.I.T. bases on Earth; the Sarispa's Teotihuacan and Giza bases could be easily reached via direct leys. The Brodgar to Giza and Brodgar to Teotihuacan lines were at one time incredibly well-travelled routes; now both those direct ley lines were never buzzed, both were heavily armed with Sarispa attacking tracking devices.

The Federation could shut down the Sarispa tracking, it was the transient, violent EMPs that posed the greatest risk to agents. Random violent flares and debilitating electromagnetic pulses rendered the travellers immobile, unable to move forwards or backwards, held within an indefensible electromagnetic attack until the agent is no more. It took the Sarispa more than a thousand years to manipulate and transform those lines from an intergalactic mode of travel to a weapon of war.

'Dharms, what did you mean, seemed a bit nuts to bust into the all-seeing eye and not see anything?' Phoenix pursued.

Dharma smiled and lifted herself onto her elbows. 'Do you remember,' she paused to think, 'must be like eight hundred years ago, we ran a rescue raid on Giza? As I recall, now it was a long time ago,' she smiled at Phoenix, 'but was it not to save you?'

'I had nearly forgotten, thanks for the reminder, and …?' He encouraged her to get to the point. The flooding memories filled his gentle face with horror.

'When I was saving you,' she winked at him, 'I got involved in an energy battle with the base Commander, it wasn't Romorph back then,' Dharma said, staring out across the rolling fields, trying to remember the name of the vicious Giza Commander.

'Secundas,' Phoenix said with a shudder. 'How could you forget his name? He was fierce.'

'Nasty piece of work as I remember it, too,' Chiron agreed, recalling the damage Secundas had brought to Earth and the Federation.

'Makes Romorph look like a pussy cat, eh Dharms?' Lynx laughed.

'Yeah a total pussy cat, one roar from Romorph and you lot tailed it through the chamber-way,' Dharma joked. It could have been Chiron, perhaps the stunning surroundings or the Grange itself, but the agents felt lighter. 'Anyway,' Dharma continued, 'I noticed the Sarispa server vault. Those are too rare to see, the only other one I've seen is at Teotihuacan. We've never been able to get past the security to access them. You need a Sarispa Commander's chip reading and a set of passwords. I saw an opportunity; let's just say a moment presented itself.'

'Really, so you actually accessed the main server?' Salva asked, intrigued and impressed.

'From the look of the intel that I did catch, it did look like it could be a main server.' Dharma said, her eyes still shut. All the better to see with. She scanned Salva. Exactly how he had passed the oracle chamber security scanner was playing on her mind. The Arcturian was still unable to view his timeline, but from what she could see as she lay on the grass at the Grange, Salva's chip was Federation standard.

Chiron smiled at Dharma. The other agents were not able to freely observe Dharma's extrasensory scanning activities, but Chiron could, ever since Dharma was very young.

'By the sound of it, we're going to need you all in tiptop order,' Chiron said, standing. 'Come, you can all check in on Rose, and we should bring you all a heal before you deploy.' Chiron led the agents down into the Limerick stone circle. They became a holographic haze and vanished into Earth's Hollow Kingdom. 'This way,' she called, leading the agents through the mirrored stone circle into the heart of the healing base.

The agents followed the trail of the healer's effervescent glow, which became more visibly vibrant in her own stunning surroundings. She guided them through lush landscape and a host of pretty white domes towards the sanctuary; Chiron's luminosity peaked as she reached the mouth of an immense quartz labyrinth.

All personnel wishing to enter the Grange healing dome were required to walk the labyrinth, an ancient intergalactic method of cleansing that's decidedly more fun than hand-wash. The agents followed the healer like a guiding wisp, all except Salva, who hesitated at the mouth. Chiron sent an encouraging energy ball in his direction. He caught the gesture and placed a foot onto the spiralling path; tepidly, he too walked the Limerick labyrinth, and when he reached the sanctuary, the entrance awoke.

Chiron and the Brodgar four peacefully passed into the Federation healing dome, a serene circular space with white walls and an otherworldly charm. A Sióg peered from behind a statue of Ashtar. The curious elemental watched the visitors as they sat down on an orbicular plinth. The faery fluttered and muttered into her hand, blew a silver substance into the oculus above, and watched.

Glowing in the warm light and silver substance, Dharma looked up and smiled. Seeing signs of a Sióg, she scanned the dome, delighted the elemental had allowed her to see. The faery whispered into the ear of a statue; the statue whispered back.

You can see Rose now, two by two, my loves, room four, Chiron linked telepathically.

The communication startled the Sióg. The frightened faery shot behind a statue of Lady Victorya.

Without hesitation or allocation, Lynx and Phoenix rose to their feet and headed to room four.

Dharma rested up on a spherical plinth, searching for signs of the Sióg, trying hard not to feel uncomfortable. The absence of Lynx and Phoenix brought back the memory of her questioning Salva's service.

'So,' she said, grappling for a lead into small talk, 'have you been to the Grange before?'

'A long time ago. I did the majority of my Federation service in Asia,' he said, sounding nervous but nonetheless eager to share.

'Asia?'

'Yeah, I was amongst the early Feds deployed there,' he said, and took her through some of his time in Asia.

'Yip,' she said, nodding towards Phoenix and Lynx, who were heading out of the healing bay. 'How's she doing?'

'Better. She's calm and stable,' Lynx said, sounding relieved.

The healers had worked wonders on Rose. She lay peacefully in the serene space. Organic dressings covered her wounded eyes, but the Federation teacher appeared visibly stabilised. Dharma scanned her old friend and mentor. Rose was back—shook up and exhausted—but she was back. She turned to the healers and thanked them.

'Thank you, my dears,' Chiron glowed back, 'Rose will be fine, given a little time.'

'Could we access a workstation?' Dharma asked as they set to exit the healing bay.

'Just in here,' Chiron said pointing to a door next to Rose's room, 'we should bring you all a heal before you deploy.'

Dharma thanked Chiron, headed to the empty station and scanned her chip. 'Brodgar field agents reporting,' she said into the activated screen.

'Bravo, Zulu Brodgar field ...' Castra's face beamed through the monitor.

'Thanks, Sir.' Dharma looked around at the other field agents. Not the normal response she receives after going AWOL.

'Must have been the main server, Dharms,' Phoenix whispered.

'Good news for you guys, we have the intel to protect you on the matrix.' Castra reported over building celebrations at Brodgar. 'Need you all back at base as soon as possible,' Castra said and disappeared from the Limerick workstation.

'Copy that!'

'Good actual day at the office, Dharms!'

'All good, my dears?' Chiron said, appearing in the doorway.

'All is good, Chiron, all is very good!' Phoenix beamed back.

'You all ready for that heal?' Chiron smiled and held the door open. 'The plinth will be fine.' The healer pointed to the circular seat positioned below the oculus. 'Who's up first?'

Silence ensued, then Lynx offered himself up. He stepped onto the plinth and stood under the free-flowing light streaming from the circular cut-out in the ceiling.

Chiron's hand fluttered with the slightest of motions, the descending light filled with phenomena. Twelve spinning spheres formed and positioned around Lynx, below his feet, above his head and all around. The vibrating orbs transcended, Lynx's body oscillated, immersed in the healing, his warm rugged features softened. Chiron lowered her palms and Lynx hovered gently back onto the plinth. The celestial lightshow faded with Lynx fully restored.

One by one, the C.I.T. agents experienced the wonders of Chiron and the oculus of light. The intergalactic healer and Aine, the Faerie Queen, watched the C.I.T. agents deploy, accompanied by twelve silver orbs.

Chapter Sixteen

The Thirteen

The once-sombre mood left no trace of existence at the Brodgar base. The incoming intel downloaded from the Giza server was nothing less than ground-breaking. The Federation had held some knowledge of the Sarispa bases, their locations and functions, while others seemed eternally evasive to them. It was similar in many ways to the task of uncovering solid up-to-date intel on the Thirteen's reptilian leaders. Constantly protected, constantly moving and rebooting, covertly shifting from positions of power to powerful positions within Earth's controlling hierarchy, through multiple millennia the Federation has sought to trace and track the Sarispa Thirteen. Lord Hitch, grand master of the reptilian order tells it like this: *We play the role of the alchemist, the illusionist, simple smoke, mirrors and optical games. Simple, yet extremely effective.*

'Intel is locked in for the Sarispa's subterranean bases.' Herc called through the building hustle in C.I.T.

'How many bases?' Castra asked, returning from the meeting room with Ashtar.

'All sixty-six of them.'

'Is Koh Ker still showing as an active base?' Ashtar enquired, taking up a station next to Herc at Terra-Command. 'Would you bring up the thermals?'

'The base is showing live subterranean activity, Sir,' Herc said, studying the active thermals for the Sarispa's covert Cambodian jungle base.

'Any indications of the base's present occupiers?'

'Going on the recent travel history, looks like it could be the Kathzers.'

'Interesting. Yes, we are aware of the Kathzers, a particularly dark Sarispa cartel.'

'Field agents are incoming.' Dorada said, informing the unit of their imminent arrival.

Four holographic figures emerged in the circle. From their solid form, four celebratory celestial spheres shot out, falling short of the shore. The buzz balls turned to stone as the celestial met with the terrestrial. The returning agents stood for a moment in the entrance. It wasn't long before ground control spotted the returning rescue squad.

'Girl, those moves were as fast as lightning! You were just a little bit, just a tiny little bit frightening.' Leo called over the spontaneous celebrations, holding a shaky cat stance.

'What's with the Kung Fu?' Phoenix asked, squeezing his way through the congregation of celebrating C.I.T. agents.

'Dharma's terra-level combat in the middle of St. Peter's Square, didn't you know? Did he not know?'

Dharma shrugged, amused by Leo and Nash's attempt to re-enact her terra-level Vatican action.

'Good work everyone, nicely done,' Castra said, ignoring the Kung Fu enactment. 'Field agents, meeting room, mission debrief.'

The agents concluded Rose's rescue report. Castra asked for Dharma's insight into the present use of the base.

'It seems the base is still functioning as an all-seeing eye,' she said, 'and in light of the uncovered intel, it would appear they have reverted back to the age of the Sphinx and assigned the base as a secret keeper again. The security was minimal, which was surprising but encouraging.'

'I did think the security was on the light side, considering the treasures held under their guard. OK, thanks guys. Let's push on.' Castra led the agents back into the dome.

'OK, settle down; time is of the essence. We want you briefed and commencing mission as soon as.'

The agents focused, hearing the audible urgency in Castra's tone.

'The newly downloaded intel from the Giza base is showing in the region of thirty-three thousand Sarispa with an "A" classification, hazardous and dangerous, already passed through the quantum gateway. One hundred thousand original-bloodline Sarispa are reading as in active service. Twenty-four thousand of those intergalactics, we are happy to report, are living harmoniously and contributing positively to the planet. The remaining seventy-six thousand original Sarispa are still fighting for the cause, pursuing karmic ownership and attempting to bring Earth into their world order. Out of those seventy-six thousand, Brodgar C.I.T. will be focusing its resources on the Thirteen.' Castra looked up from the screen. 'Which, thanks to Brodgar,' he turned to acknowledge Dharma, 'the Federation now has solid up-to-date intel. Brodgar C.I.T. has been assigned to pass four of the Thirteen through the quantum gateway.'

'Four of them?' Leo blurted, forgetting to filter, 'that's a bit flippen hefty, Castra.'

'It might be hefty, Leo, but that's what we've assigned; take it up with the Council of Twelve if you've got issues.' Castra's tone sounded sterner than his expression. 'OK, let's take you through an update on the Thirteen.' The Commander continued, 'Elflock, second in command after Hitch, is as we speak in the processes of rebooting. As of now, we have no confirmed intel on Elflock's reboot, who, where or when we do not know. Elflock traditionally walks into a host body, as do most of the Thirteen, but with no data recorded within the downloaded intel, perhaps even the Sarispa don't know who, where or when.'

The images on their screens switched up. Elflock was replaced by a middle-aged humanoid male. 'OK, Thore. Traditionally, Thore is the Thirteen assigned to oversee control and manipulation via news and popular media feeds. The Sarispa's global media stronghold is largely down to Thore. Their grip has slipped in recent years, but overall, the Sarispa still control the planet's mainstream news and media. Mystery Hill C.I.T. has been assigned to perform Thore's quantum lockdown.'

The image of the media ringleader was replaced by the Sarispa men and women of science.

'Beckett Normandy, Simon Hedge and Phinehas Coatl, three Sarispa scientists to ensure the planet develops and supports the molecular formula of their intergalactic race. Intel is showing the three scientists are based, for the time being, at the Sarispa sub-base in Geneva. Brodgar C.I.T. has been assigned to Normandy, Hedge and Coatl.' Castra glanced up from his screen, sensing a tangible shift around the dome.

'The Sarispa scientists hold unthinkable possibilities: the technology, the ability and the historic temperament of the intergalactic reptilian race is sadly evident throughout the multiverse.'

The images of the three dark Sarispa scientists dissolved, replaced by the images of a humanoid man and woman.

'Helga and Finscar. Helga was placed through the quantum gateway by none other than our very own Leo and Nash.' Castra saluted the duo. 'Her place in the Thirteen has since been walked in by a Sarispa general; second-generation Helga looks and sounds the same as the first.'

'Really?' Nash said, making a face.

'Still to this day, the only Sarispa Thirteen to be successfully passed through the quantum gateway.' Leo said, his gaze setting off into the distance, recalling the yearlong track and weeklong battle. The duo eventually outwitted Helga, albeit quite accidentally.

'Finscar and second-generation Helga are openly active, with the aid of their dark cartel of global toxic terrorists. Finscar and Helga are responsible for numerous global atrocities and genocides. At the moment, their favourite concern appears to be purging the planet of all natural organisms via seed mutation and modification. Their seed is forced and farming suicide. Cellular disease is on the increase; natural pollination and regeneration is on the decline. Finscar, Helga and their crusading cartel are highly dangerous. Should you come into contact, approach with extreme caution.' Finscar and Helga disappeared from the agents' screens, replaced by the image of an almost luminous-looking humanoid.

'Portland, the Thirteen's master political leader. His throne of power shifts, but he seems relatively comfortable nestled into the inverted pentagram.' Castra said, glancing at the agents. 'Mystery Hill has been assigned to pass Portland through the gateway.'

'The Hill are gonna be busy,' Leo said, sounding relieved that Brodgar had not been assigned to Hitch's political puppet. Portland was well-known to the long-serving Federation agents, and through his many reboots, Hitler to name but one, he has slipped the keys of nations through cracks in the cosmos.

'OK, Frang the fear monger,' Castra introduced the round, short humanoid uploading onto their screens. 'Nothing sells your war quicker than terrifying propaganda. Frang is always strategically placed, always poised to detonate, paraded on Sarispa run media, and before you know it, the planet's inhabitants are suctioned into a subconscious pocket of fear. Minds are easily moulded when filled with fear. He is a dynamic, dramatic and commonly used weapon of war. Hiwasun C.I.T. have been assigned to gateway Frang the fear monger.'

'Unlucky lads.' Phoenix said, commiserating with the Korean unit, secretly celebrating he would not be part of Frang's undoubtedly fierce quantum lockdown.

'General Syone, as he's been known in recent years, has by the looks of the downloaded intel focused his military attention on the Middle East, although we could always presuppose his presence would pop up when and where a military mix-up was needed. Qasr Abu C.I.T. has been assigned to Syone's quantum lockdown.

'OK, Benedito,' Castra introduced a contorted, strange-looking man on their screens. 'Known for installing religion and distorting history, dark, dangerous and highly magical. Brazilian unit, Amapa C.I.T. has been assigned to perform Benedito's quantum lockdown.' The haunting image of the Thirteen faded, replaced by a reptilian humanoid monarch. 'OK, Gothburg. The Sarispa sovereign has been passed to Stonehenge C.I.T. Ladies and gentlemen,' Castra took to his feet, 'we have left the best till last.'

Gothburg faded, replaced by the evil embodiment of the ancient dark order. 'Lord Hitch.'

The air in the dome froze, and through a contortion in the cosmos, an oversized spider forced its way into C.I.T. The field agents shot stuns at the invading intergalactic insect; the spider morphed into a dark, hairy orb and rolled back through the closing crack. With a whitewashing of conjoined energy, the agents sealed the spot the sent spider had crept into the dome.

'Man, I hate it when that happens,' Phoenix cringed, slumping back down into his station.

The agents' distracted attention returned to the contorted vision on their screens, perhaps preferring the view of the un-welcomed arachnid to the malevolent reptilian humanoid sleekly staring back at them. The thin veil of Hitch's humanoid exterior made no real attempt to disguise his true and proud reptilian heritage. The obvious elongated skull was emphasized by the balding head, gaunt lizard face and evil all-seeing eyes.

'And there he is folks, sitting on the top of the Sarispa food chain, grand master of the reptilian order, wealthiest being on the planet, Lord Hitch.' Castra looked around at the unit, the veterans and newbies alike, scanned the space for signs of further invading aides, arachnid or otherwise. Castra continued, confident that the field agents had sealed the dome from further inquisitive visitors. 'Hitch's control and planetary domination comes in the form of money. He holds a majority share in nearly all of Earth's financial systems and institutions. Hitch likes to think this equates to planetary ownership.' Castra took a deep breath. Filled with air and courage, he announced, 'Brodgar C.I.T. has been assigned to pass Hitch through the quantum gateway.'

'You are actually kidding, Castra. Hitch is one of our allocated Thirteen?' Leo blurted, disbelief debilitating his filter again.

'Sadly, he is not,' Ashtar said, concurring with Castra.

'Forgot you were there, Commander. Sorry, but really?'

'Brodgar C.I.T ...' Castra continued, leaving little space for a Leo-led uprising, 'has been assigned to pass Hitch and the scientists, Beckett Normandy, Simon Hedge and Phinehas Coatl, through the quantum gateway.'

'The scientists and Hitch! Do we really have the resources to take on four of the Thirteen?' Leo continued, not quite ready to sit down. The dome fell silent and expectant.

'The Council of Twelve have complete faith Brodgar holds within it both the wisdom and the will. The assignment of the mission was written in stone a very long time ago.' Ashtar spoke and rose; with his rise, Leo backed down. 'Field agents, it is time. The Sarispa scientists.'

'All up-to-date maps and intel are downloaded onto your chips.' Castra told the deploying field agents. 'Look, when you come into contact with the scientists, do us all a favour and don't enter into combat,' he said, looking directly at Dharma. 'It's not Romorph you're dealing with now. Normandy, Hedge and Coatl are dark and deadly; remember, if the body dies, if they impale their chip they will return to the matrix reboot and occupy an awaiting host, and we're back to square one.'

Each of the experienced Earth agents had at one time or another a Thirteen within their grasp, poised to pass them through the quantum gateway, only to lose them or the gateway. The very last thing the leaders of the reptilian order wanted was to be passed through the gateway; once the door was closed, so was their quantum passage to Earth. The Federation has watched lifetime after lifetime, reboot after reboot; the Thirteen amassed more, controlled more, became ever more deadly and ever closer to complete planetary domination.

'We've got this, chief,' Dharma said, setting off along the chamber-way towards the Ring of Brodgar.

'Remember,' Castra shouted from outside the stone circle, 'they won't let any of you stand in their way.'

'Can't hear you, what did you say?' Dharma shouted back.

'Who's mission Alpha?' Phoenix asked, preparing to travel.

'Dharma.' Castra shouted back, bouncing from foot to foot, a combination of nervous energy and Arctic chills.

'Good to go?' Dharma asked, glancing around at the field agents.

The physical form of the four disappeared. Four pools of silvery liquid appeared in the spot where the agents entered the matrix. Castra clocked the unusual indicator. Without inspecting the substance any closer, he headed back into C.I.T.

'Field agents have just exited the matrix in Geneva.' Herc called as Castra re-entered the dome.

'Let me know when we lose them.'

'Signal is holding for now.'

'Perfect.' Castra said, settling into his station. 'Dorada, focus on the G.C.N.R. security systems, any fluctuations, alert ground and field. Alpha-Omega, follow up every irregularity with and around your agents' code; even the smallest fluctuation could indicate an unfolding situation.' Castra's attention was drawn towards the dome's illuminating entrance.

The Commander sanctioned the visitation request. The shadows of two spacemen filled the dome. The ground agents looked up, distracted by the intergalactics carrying canisters. The special agents took a trip around the Ring of Brodgar, examined the newly sprung galactic geysers and gathered the travel residue—liquid mercury—for analysis.

Chapter Seventeen

Masters of Time and Space

Deep below Europe's largest mountain range are twenty thousand secret bunkers and the planet's largest subterranean scientific research network. It apparently makes real sense, if you have the ability to cause intergalactic devastation, you also have the resources to hide from it, at least for a heartbeat, which is just long enough for the masters of time and space to evacuate to a planet not affected by their devastation. The Sarispa don't really desire to obliterate Earth; the ancient order do not consider themselves intergalactic beings, to them, they are Earth's original inhabitants, to them, they are home. If the Thirteen felt under pressure, felt that they were losing control of Earth, then it's thought the

Sarispa may attempt to take out Earth. If they can't have it, no one will.

The Council of Twelve believes damage to time and space, cosmic manipulation and war are greater risks to Earth than outright planetary obliteration; sadly, other systems have not been quite so fortunate. After inciting war on Alpha Centauri, the Sarispa scientists brutally annihilated the peaceful advanced system. Without warning, Centauri was removed from the multiverse, the spirit of the system. The only remnants of the once-glorious galaxy rests within the astral graveyard. The notorious reptilian scientists hold the ability to not only obliterate your galaxy, but with their ever-expanding capabilities, they could, very soon, pop it back again.

The field agents had been an epitome of stealth for the first thirty minutes of cold dark tunnels leading them into the Sarispa's Global Centre for Nuclear Research, Geneva base. Dharma brought the unit to a halt, scanned the base and collated her live remote view.

'Beckett Normandy is situated within his living quarters,' Dharma said, updating the unit, 'he's closest to our location; looks like

Normandy's up first. Phinehas Coatl,' Dharma's body gave an involuntary shudder, 'is playing with dark matter in research room six.' The remote view of the Sarispa scientist told like a modern-day horror story, the type of tale that would be pieced together way after the fact. 'Hedge is working close to the Collider, it's too risky. Normandy, Coatl, then check Hedge's location again, and we'll take it from there.'

The agents set off through the seemingly endless tunnels until gradually the passageways became smaller and more domesticated. The tunnels leading to the base had so far been devoid of any Sarispa, as was anticipated, but signs of life began hitting their senses.

The unit cautiously approached the entrance to a catering area. 'Quickest route to Normandy's quarters is through there.' Dharma said pointing towards the dining room. She disappeared behind the kitchen's double swing door, reappearing moments later with four sets of chef whites.

The thirty or so dining Sarispa sounded more like a hundred and thirty: rising volumes, competing dialects, and egos craving supremacy tightened the eating space. The stark walls and clinical dining furniture could not disguise the food-like substances being consumed. The agents covertly manoeuvred through the G.C.N.R. dining room, lifting and shifting abandoned plastic plates from one end to the other end of the dining area.

'At least they eat their own freaky frankenfood.' Phoenix muttered as the agents, still dressed in chef whites, set course towards Beckett Normandy's living quarters.

The passageways became an increasing hustle of passing personnel, mostly scientists and technicians heading for lunch. The agents moved relatively assured through the Sarispa base, concealing energy shields disguising their true identity. At one point, a huddle of kitchen staff approached the unit, pausing and observing, before continuing on their way. Lynx and Salva thought for sure they were busted. Dharma utilised the encounter and surreptitiously scanned and downloaded intel from the slightly confused kitchen staff.

The agents approached Normandy's quarters undetected. The entrance was as they had assumed, armed steel with a biometric iris scanner, G.N.C.R. standard. Dharma positioned herself in front of the reptilian leader's doorway and pressed the intercom.

'Yes.'

'Kitchen delivery, Sir.' Dharma replied in a voice that was not her own, but borrowed from a kitchen porter. The iris scanner activated and took an infrared reading of the porters' projected vision. The door to Normandy's quarters opened.

A bright light growing in Dharma's palms shot across the scientist's quarters. The stun engulfed Normandy. The impenetrable sphere locked the scientist down before he had time to react. The moment was massive for Dharma, and massive for the multiverse. Thousands of years of tracking, tracing, and missing mostly by a mile had led to this moment. Dharma aligned herself and energetically prepared to open the quantum gateway.

A minuscule sphere of light grew in her hands, and simultaneously, deep within the cosmos, a dimensional triangle awakened. Dharma guided the multidimensional transcendent light show. An emerging kaleidoscope of colour and geometric shapes signalled that the gateway was almost fully awakened. The gateway, permitting instant quantum displacement, complete quantum lockdown, engulfed Becket Normandy. The multidimensional triangle lit like a vibrant rainbow; optical phenomena flooded the scientist's quarters. The quantum gateway reached its dimensional destination, the eleventh dimension. With both hands and all her will, the Arcturian locked the stunned scientist into the gateway.

The intergalactic vortex exploded, two tetrahedrons spun, blinding effervescent light warped, and Beckett Normandy's existence on Earth shut down with the gateway. The seismic silence was broken by the G.N.C.R. alarms ringing out.

'Lynx, get us out of here,' Dharma said staggering to keep a firm footing. The extended energy had been more than she had anticipated. Lynx caught her before she fell and led the agents into the matrix.

Almost instantly, the unit returned to terra level. Lynx rested Dharma against a tree. No one had anticipated or could have predicted the extreme electromagnetic reaction she was experiencing. As she was, it was too dangerous for her to travel.

'Why did you bring us here, Lynx?' Dharma asked, trying to focus.

'Salva suggested it. Dharms, we've only got a few minutes before the Sarispa pick us up, do you think you'll be OK to travel?'

'A pay-it-forward apology, is that what this is?' She mumbled, trying to walk towards a pool of water.

'OK, let's sit you back here ...'

Dharma ignored Lynx's attempts to guide her back to the cover of the tree and continued to stagger towards a water feature pool. 'Look at this place!' she said, sitting at the water's edge. She took her boots off, dipping her feet into the pool. Instantly, her vitals began to balance out.

'What the hell, Dharma ... get back here!' Lynx panicked as she spectacularly broke cover, wading through the water towards the spherical sculpture.

'Did you know this was created by one of Portland's favourite Sarispa artists?' Dharma stood in the middle of the pool, releasing the potentially deadly electromagnetic surges, studying the embellished globe and brushing a finger over the sculpture of the Earth's grid.

'Dharms,' Lynx tried to cajole her back to the water's edge, 'come sit down by the tree, rest for a bit.'

Dharma ignored Lynx's suggestion and continued to study the intricate metal sculptures worked into the sphere. The visual depiction of the planet's energetic grid helped ground the intergalactic being.

Suspicious shapes began shifting in the rising mist. Thirteen vaporous emanations hauntingly surrounded the Arcturian. Dharma shut down the deep-space psychic connection to gateway eleven and released the override of energy. Anchored from her interdimensional journey, she sent the eerie galactic gathering on their way.

She sat down at the water's edge and put her socks and boots back on. 'I'm good to go,' she said, terra firm and ready to travel.

'What do you think, is she OK to travel?' Salva quietly asked, watching her from the cover of the tree.

'She'll be fine; she's tough, tougher than you think.'

Salva's line of vision was drawn from Dharma. A small telling bird sent to spy caught his eye.

'We've got to go,' Salva said, standing, signalling it was the time to deploy. Dharma and Lynx caught the gesture. 'They know we're here,' Salva said, watching the miniature owl fly back towards the Union of Nations buildings.

***

'Agents have entered the matrix, repeat, agents have deployed from Sarispa soil and are heading through France,' Herc called, updating the C.I.T. ground agents.

'Send me their projected coordinates, Herc,' Castra asked, watching the agents' ternaries. 'Dharma's floundering, she's losing consciousness. What's the closest Federation base to their present coordinates?'

'Grotto of Massabieleis is the closest healing base, and it looks like that's where they're heading.'

An unconscious agent on the matrix is an open agent. If an agent's ternaries are being followed and the agent becomes unconscious on the matrix, they are in real-time danger of being attacked or abducted. Unlike the ley lines, which need to be buzzed from one vortex to another, the matrix can be entered and exited at will. Castra sent an alert to Lady Maria, who already knew that the field agents were en route.

Chapter Eighteen

Tea and Sanctuary

An ethereal figure held vigil and poured in preparation. Steam from a pot of hot tea brought a whimsical warmth to the homely subterranean space. The vibrant vapours danced in sync with an incoming haze. Through the vapours and the haze, four apparitions emerged. The emanations took shape and laid Dharma's unconscious torso onto a waning-moon sofa.

The lady held a steaming cup of tea just below Dharma's nose and gestured to her guests to rest up on the lunar loungers.

'Have some tea, cake?'

'Thank you, Lady Maria.' Salva bowed, graciously accepting the tea and respite.

'What happened?' Dharma asked, slowly coming to, struggling to pull herself up.

'Welcome back my love, rest up,' Maria said, helping Dharma find a comfortable position. 'As you passed one of the reptilian bloodlines through the quantum gateway, an essence of your equilibrium lost balance. Your being is somehow linking to the shift, and as the effects of the diminished bloodline continue to reverberate through humanity, so does your connection to it. We have so little experience of passing the Thirteen through the gateway, we are learning by your example.'

The fog had started to shift from Dharma's mind and vision. The hot, sweet tea regenerated her spirit, yet Maria was still surrounded by a haze.

'Your shields and protection we now know are inadequate, but easily remedied,' Maria said, smiling at Dharma. 'Drink up, plenty more tea in the pot.'

'Lady Maria, can we check in with Brodgar on your system?' Lynx asked. Maria gestured for him to continue. He scanned his wrist across the round table and a workstation activated, showing a live feed from Brodgar C.I.T.

'Lady Maria,' Castra said, his face coming into focus on the monitor, 'thank you for taking in my agents. Well done, Alpha-Omega.'

'Commander Castra, always a joy to help. Your unit is presently sipping my hand-blended tea.'

'Perfect, thank you. Maria, we are watching Dharma's stats from our side. We can see her vitals are balancing out; our concern is putting her back out in the field too quickly.'

'A little more tea, a shower in my cavern, fresh shields and Dharma will be as good as new.'

'Drink up, Dharms!' Leo's voice rang through the monitor.

'Indeed, drink up,' Maria agreed. 'A monumental success has taken place. I see potential global change and intergalactic transformation from the banishment of one single soul, one thirteenth of the reigning bloodlines diminished.'

'Yes, the stats are looking good so far, Lady Maria.' Castra said, concurring with Maria's vision.

'How you doing, Dharms?'

'Getting there, Leo.'

'OK. Shower and shields,' Castra said, 'we'll clear the channel before the Sarispa pick up a trace. Over and out.'

'Maria,' Dharma said, finishing the tea in her cup, 'may I?' She pointed towards a carved wooden door.

'Please do. I will walk with you.' Lady Maria led Dharma out of the subterranean living room through a long chamber-way. The space gradually became a blended vision of Maria's home and the heart of Mother Nature. 'Dharma.' Maria said, reaching out for her hands as they approached the cavern. The women closed their eyes and watched shared visions—puzzle pieces brought together by their joint presence. The sounds of free-flowing water became more audible and the seeing concluded.

Dharma left Maria in the chamber-way and walked through the haematite archway into the subterranean crystal cavern. Images of light and tranquillity danced around the glistening walls and free-flowing waterfalls. She stepped into the warm pool and swam to the falls; instantly, the residual connection to Normandy's gateway began to disperse.

Maria walked back towards the living room, reflecting on a recalling vision, a vision that told of Dharma's Federation mission many moons ago. The incarnations of Maria and Dharma had crossed paths on many lifetimes. Within this present reboot, they were initially brought together when Lady Maria was visited by a group of young Federation children, much like a school outing. The children took a tour, experienced the wonders of a swim and shower in the subterranean crystal cavern, then afterwards the children enjoyed the enchanting delights of Maria's blended tea and homemade cake. She recalled watching the children laughing and chattering. 'The secret,' she had told them, 'is in the water.'

The children giggled—most of the children, but not all. A long, almost gangly girl, bright red hair cut into a square, sat stony silent, choosing not to interact with the other intergalactic children. The girl had intrigued Maria; she understood the spoken language but chose not to communicate within the frequency. Instead, the young girl followed the surrounding activity by watching visions and communicating telepathically. It was not entirely unusual for intergalactic children to relate in this way; many will experience much like that, but still Maria watched. That evening, Ashtar arrived as the children set to depart.

'That is also our insights into Dharma,' Ashtar had told Maria. 'We know that her role is integral, but even we cannot know all. It would be both unwise and unsafe.'

'I have looked into Dharma's reboot history and ancestral lines, I take it that you too have viewed them. Do you hold this knowledge also?' Maria asked.

'Dharma has elected and been selected to serve, this much I know, perhaps she will play an integral role only time will tell.'

'The ancestral links she holds alone bring danger, peril comes with this power as we both know.'

'I see the potential and know the risk; Dharma has continually chosen to serve reboot after reboot, regardless of ancestors or indeed, the dangers involved.' Ashtar had said, rising reluctantly out of Maria's comfortable lunar couch. 'With the knowledge of what is known, with the power and potential she holds, it would be wise for us both to follow the unfoldment of Dharma's path.' Ashtar set to depart. 'Perhaps it is best for all concerned if this information is not openly known.'

Lady Maria bowed and the commune concluded. Maria and Ashtar often discussed Dharma's developments; when she reached a milestone, completed a program of training or a particular mission, it was acknowledged. Maria arrived back in the Lourdes living room, releasing the replaying memories before entering, and when she did, the mood was light. Lynx and Salva drank tea and ate cake, watching Phoenix re-enact Dharma's simple, yet as Phoenix put it, 'genius' entrance into Beckett Normandy's quarters, and for the grand finale, the spectacular quantum lockdown of the Sarispa scientist.

'Bravo, Phoenix!' Maria applauded and took her familiar spot on the lunar lounger. 'Encore ...' she called, curled up with a cup of tea.

***

Thirty centimetres of air existed between Dharma and the quartz cavern floor. Her levitating figure arched gently backwards, like the swan's dance upon the lake moving through the shades of her own being. Allowing her shadow to rise and dance, from dark to light, light to dark, and in that moment of duality the intergalactic agent disconnected from Normandy's quantum lockdown.

'You lot ready for number two?' she asked, appearing in the doorway of Lady Maria's living room.

'Bring it on!' Phoenix said, jumping to his feet, ready for action.

'Just one or two final matters before you deploy.' Maria said, positioning the agents to be scanned and protected. A shield of pure white light grew beyond Lady Maria's being; engulfing Salva, surrounding Lynx, it shielded Phoenix and cloaked Dharma. 'They should,' she said, checking the shields, 'hold you through the matrix.' Maria noticed a flaw, a minuscule gap in Salva's shield. With the slightest of breaths, her light filled the void. 'Good. Yes, that should do it, the shields should keep you safe on the matrix and make it more difficult for you to be tracked, traced and attacked from a distance. Sadly, they will not hold out any direct attacks from The Thirteen, but they should help protect you from extreme quantum-magnetic reactions. If the opportunity arises and you're positioned to place another Thirteen through the quantum gateway, reactions should hopefully be lessened.'

'Well all good then.' Phoenix said, delighted at the thought of not being tracked, traced or attacked from a distance. The fact that those or any other shields would not hold out a deadly attack from a Thirteen had either not sunk in, or he was just happy to skip that part.

Maria scanned her wrist across the table, activating a holographic globe. 'Coatl and Hedge are no longer at the Geneva base; you may need to switch up your flight-suit settings.' Maria said, pointing to the southern snow-capped continent.

'Antarctica, really?' Phoenix beamed at Maria. 'We hardly ever get to go there.'

'I've been loads of times,' Lynx said, looking a bit confused.

'Same.' Dharma smiled.

'Yip, me too.' Salva nodded.

'Just me then ...'

'I'm sure you're not alone, Phoenix.' Maria smiled and expanded the hovering globe. 'Head Northwest. The safest route will be via Villers-sur-Mer, a minor vortex, but it will allow you to travel the Prime Meridian without alerting the Sarispa. Exit the matrix as soon as you hit the Antarctica mainland. The closer you are to the pole, the higher the risk of being pulled into the open vortex. You will feel a distinct vibrational shift as you approach the Antarctic outer perimeter. Your Alpha, which I presume is still Dharma?' Maria glanced at Dharma, who tilted her head in supposed agreement. 'Dharma will slow down the unit's travel speed as soon as you enter the outer circle, until you reach land. A stealth craft will be waiting to take you within a four-mile radius of the Sarispa base. The craft won't travel any further toward the pole.'

'Will the craft lift us at the same drop-off coordinates?' Dharma asked, double-checking the return journey.

'They will. You'll have a four-hour turnaround. If you do not make your return within the designated time, the craft will return to its planet of origin and await further orders. Do you all have the maps and intel downloads for the base?'

The agents closed their eyes and viewed the downloaded intel and maps covering the Sarispa's Antarctic base.

'Full and present data,' Dharma, Lynx and Phoenix called in unison.

'I'm missing portions of the maps, Lady Maria.' Salva said, scanning the Antarctic intel stored in his chip.

Maria hovered a finger over Salva's chip. Full and complete maps of the Antarctic base passed from Maria to Salva. Visions flowed from Salva to Maria: dark images of ancient times, beginnings and endings, complicated creations, massacres, floods and death.

Maria pulled away. 'You have the maps, my love.'

Chapter Nineteen

Antarctic Adventures

Four hovering figures cast rainbows across infinite sheets of white snow. The spectral reflection failed to penetrate the invisibility shield of the awaiting stealth craft. The agents were suctioned into the ship's gravitational propulsion, passed through an open hatch and entered the awaiting craft.

'Whoa, cool ship! What we riding today, lads?' Phoenix enthused and reluctantly took a seat in the passenger bay.

'Just your standard multi-crew transporter, nothing exciting. Let me help you with that.' The entirely blue copilot helped Phoenix buckle up.

'Agents secure?' the pilot asked, preparing to take to flight.

'Secure.'

The view from the helm was almost identical when the craft momentarily displaced from one point to another.

'Good job guys, slick.' Phoenix said, fumbling to set himself free from the harness and check out the helm.

'Stay in the passenger bay,' the co-pilot said defensively, taking to his feet.

The pilot spun his flight chair to face the agents. His form, not at all Earthly humanoid, but distinctly intergalactic, indicated the craft and crew had temporally transported from an interstellar base, most probably Europa. 'Our orders are to await your return at these coordinates for a period of four Earth hours. If you do not return within this given time, we will return to base. Should our activity be detected, we will displace and return when a window of opportunity opens.' The chalk-white captain cast charcoal eyes over the agents' unprepared outerwear.

Dharma, Lynx and Salva registered the silent observation and switched up their flight suit settings. They stood head-to-toe white and weather-proofed, protected from the extreme weather conditions, and hopefully providing a covert entrance to the Sarispa base.

Dharma nudged Phoenix. He lifted the cuff of his suit and selected the Antarctic variant. The unit stood snowsuit-ready on the ship's underbelly hatch. The hatch disappeared and snow appeared. The agents hovered, held in a vacuum, as the craft lowered them towards land. They looked upward as they reached terra level but saw nothing except white Antarctic sky.

The unit moved out in silence, managing a steady pace though the extreme conditions: thick snow and ice under foot, in freezing blizzards with almost zero visibility.

Dharma signalled for the unit to halt. With her eyes closed, she checked their coordinates. 'We've routed too far west,' she called over the rasping southern wind, aligning her internal compass. 'We're less than a mile out from the base. We'll attempt primary entry via the transport hangar,' she said and signalled for the unit to head out.

'Pyramids, twelve o'clock,' Salva said, pointing towards three emerging snow-covered mounds. 'The mark of Elflock, look—the Earth's grid and a pyramid.' The unit fell to the ground. As the pyramids became more visible, so did the giant half-humanoid, half-eagle guards.

Through an unknowing eye the pyramids may appear as snow-covered mountains, but those that seek will see, and what the agents saw were three pyramids embellished with the crest of their canny creator, Elflock.

'Ripsaw patrol en route,' Dharma said, scanning the area. The agents laid low; the patrol passed and entered the hangar. The guards moved back into position and continued pacing the entrance, like oversized clockwork canaries. 'Stuns on three.' Dharma gave the command. Simultaneously, four flashes of light locked down the unsuspecting Anunnaki guards.

The agents moved out and entered the Sarispa Antarctic base. A spacecraft and an armed tank dominated the entrance to the huge hangar. Beyond the adroit rows of ripsaws and ski buggies, a shadow lingered.

A Sarispa technician was inspecting the returned ripsaw; satisfied, they set off through a doorway at the rear of the hangar. Dharma signalled for the unit to split up. She and Lynx reached the length of the hangar only to realise Phoenix and Salva were still rooted at the entrance, transfixed by the craft.

'Patrolling drones in the chamber-way covering the entrance to the base—approximately six.' Dharma whispered once Phoenix and Salva had managed to join them at the entrance to the chamber-way leading the unit down into the base.

The door released from the lock, Lynx kicked it wide open and flashes lit the dark chamber-way.

'Clear.'

The agents moved out, crushing the stunned micro-pentagon robotic spies at the end of the chamber-way. Dharma halted the unit and scanned beyond the door, into the base ahead.

'Anunnaki guards.'

'Coatl and Hedge's quarters, are you looking there?' Lynx said, shuddering at the remote view of the army of security protecting the Sarispa scientists. 'We could turn back, bring in more agents?' Lynx suggested, feeling the suction of a Sarispa snare.

'That's what they want us to do: the more agents we bring in, the more they have to bring down.' Dharma's words were fuelled. She had watched and seen the Sarispa's tactics time and time again. It would take a lot more than a huddle of ancient Anunnaki to make her run for the hills. 'At the end of the great hall, the base splits off into two sections,' she said. 'The northwestern side leads to laboratories and living quarters, the northeastern side to a pentagram space; Coatl and Hedge's quarters are accessed via the pentagram. Blend, take to the ceiling and run, fast.'

Salva sent a surge into the entrance security system, and one by one, the agents entered the heart of the Sarispa Antarctic base, simultaneously leaping and landing on the ceiling of the great hall.

The vision of what they had seen, the amount of Anunnaki they had been shown, had been kind to their sensibilities. The Anunnaki present at the base, guarding the polar pyramid, reached very much beyond their imaginations.

The once-peaceful mining race, thirty-nine thousand light years from home, visited Earth post-comet Typhon. The constellation leapers from Capricornus caught sight of the comet's tail and followed the trail. Magnificent minerals are mined post-devastation; between ages is a prosperous period for those seeking treasure and control. The Anunnaki were not the only intergalactic visitors to Earth at the dawn of the new age. Reptilian travellers, without a home to call their own, ensnared the once-noble winged species. The Anunnaki grew dark in their enslavement, in their part in the Sarispa pseudo-populating primate scheme.

From the corner of her eye, Dharma watched Salva. He jumped down off the ornate ceiling, held the leap mid-air, narrowly avoiding the searching wings of Anunnaki guards closing in on him. The deeper into the great hall the agents went, the more unsettled the Anunnaki became. Sensing the presence of the Federation, wings spanned out, searching for the invaders. Cold, shrilling shrieks sounded through tongues tasting the air; the Anunnaki looked but could not see.

A General emerged from the parting crowd. 'They are here.'

Dharma dodged the wings of the suspicious leader reaching out just below her head. 'Spread out, search the entire base,' he said, still standing directly under Dharma, tasting the air around her, sensing her presence. The General reached his wings to the area where she was.

Lynx, Salva and Phoenix readied to stun the General. Dharma held her breath, shielded her presence and prepared to fire at the ancient leader of the Anunnaki, when she felt an unexpected object resting in the palm of her hand. A golden nugget appeared, she instinctively knew what to do.

To the Anunnaki, there is no greater treasure or pleasure than gold. Dharma threw the gold nugget out into the great hall and ran along the ceiling towards the unit. The Anunnaki General scrambled like a cold turkey addict after the precious metal.

Dharma reached the unit and scanned the area for Phinehas Coatl and Simon Hedge. Both were poised to reboot, and both were surrounded by Bloods; vicious, mutated intergalactic hybrid bodyguards.

Salva caught Dharma's eye as she set to decipher, at a distance, the security system protecting the scientists' quarters. He shook his head. The entrance security was a combination of Blood and Anunnaki technology; if your molecular make-up did not align with either of those species, a surreptitious entrance to the scientists' safe space was highly unlikely.

Another golden nugget appeared in Dharma's hand. Lynx looked at his hand, then Salva, and Phoenix, too. Each of them held a surprising nugget in the palms of their hands. The agents glanced at one another and knew. Dharma threw the nugget; it tumbled and landed in the heart of the pentagram. Lynx's landed just beyond Dharma's, Salva's beyond his. Phoenix aimed, fired and completed the nugget trail leading to Coatl's door. The Anunnaki General followed the line of gold, and the agents followed the general, resting on the ceiling above him as he pressed the intercom.

'My lady, we are experiencing unusual activity in the base.'

'What unusual activity?' Coatl's voice shook through the intercom.

The entrance security scanner activated, confirmed the General's identity and unlocked.

'General, what unusual activity?' Coatl snapped as he stepped into the scientist's quarters.

The C.I.T. agents silently manoeuvred over the door's frame and quietly crawled onto the ceiling of Coatl's quarters. Unnerved and sensing the Federation, Coatl's hand was held high: an impaling metal spike where a finger had once been was positioned to penetrate her chip.

Coatl's quarters filled with light. Fast-firing shots locked down the ancient scientist. Blinded by the stuns and before they had time to decipher where to fire, the Bloods and Anunnaki General were stunned.

You are too late, Federation freaks. Coatl, frozen and unable to move, still managed to force telepathic messages into the agents' minds. *I have created a parallel universe, I is now we!*

The unit flipped down from the ceiling and surrounded the Sarispa scientist.

'Not a problem, Phinehas, I'm happy to come shut you down, whenever, wherever ...' Dharma said, and energetically prepared. The building energy in the palms of her hands birthed a miniature tetrahedron. The celestial gateway commenced its multidimensional journey.

Biggest mistake you've ever made, Arcturian. It's not too late to break down the gateway. The ancient alien's face, as frozen at it was, became frenzied. *Lady Maria?*

Coatl's cold call sent shivers through the agents.

I sense you here on Sarispa soil. I am honoured, Lady Maria, but I tell you when it's done! Coatl fought off the Federation stun, held high her claw and pierced it into her chip.

The gateway's interdimensional growth stopped. Coatl disappeared and returned to the matrix to reboot.

'Son of a …' Dharma spun on the spot, firing stun after stun randomly around the scientist quarters, then turned to the awakening Bloods and General and aimed. 'That should hold them for now,' she said, still not looking at the other agents. 'Hedge?'

'Sounds like a plan.' Lynx said encouragingly.

The unit stormed Hedge's quarters and stunned the heavy guard of Bloods. A light grew in Dharma's palms, and the quantum gateway commenced its celestial journey through the dimensions. Hedge did not protest as Coatl had. His self-satisfied, unperturbed look fuelled the process for Dharma. Spinning tetrahedrons engulfed the ancient Sarispa scientist and motioned him through the dimensional realms of the multiverse. Dharma willed the gateway to transcend, to journey beyond the earthly realms, beyond time and space. Shifting through the sixth dimension onto the seventh, the eighth to the ninth, the quantum gateway transcended from the tenth dimension to the eleventh. The dark multiverse manipulator reached Dharma's desired dimensional destination. The gateway imploded, warped, and then faded.

The Sarispa scientist was eternally locked down, here and now within this reality of Earth, Simon Hedge will never again walk among you. Cracks appeared where moments before the Sarispa scientist stood.

Dharma vibrated like a hollow vacuum, consumed by the interdimensional lockdown. Salva swept in behind her, catching her before she hit the floor. The chamber shook. The agents staggered as paintings, sculptures and micro particle manipulators flew across the room.

'Let's get the hell out of here,' Lynx said, lifting Dharma from Salva's support. 'Ready to roll?' he asked, glancing at Phoenix and Salva. Unable to ceiling run with an agent on his back, they would have to fight their way through the Anunnaki.

'Already rolling, chief,' Phoenix said, staring intently at the door, ready for whatever lay behind it.

Lynx gave Salva the go-ahead. Salva fired at the security scanner and the door unlocked.

'What the …' Lynx said, edging slowly forward, scanning the space. 'Clear, move out?'

The unit ran through the empty pentagram space, slowing down before entering the great hall. Lynx struggled to manoeuvre with Dharma saddled over his shoulder, but awkwardly positioned himself to look out into the base. He pulled back, astonished. Again, he looked out; through the great hall, towards the hangar was clear. The eastern wing leading to the laboratories and living quarters was not. Lynx motioned for Phoenix and Salva to view the sight.

Hundreds of enslaved ancient Anunnaki surrounded an old Nazi train. Inside the train was gold. Stolen gold and lots of it, taken from the Anunnaki many moons ago. A final act of disempowerment from the Sarispa. The once great, now enslaved race bowed to the gold. A growing tidal wave of white light, the source unseen, engulfed the train and the Anunnaki. The train, the gold and the travelling miners disappeared in a flooding wash of light.

The Anunnaki returned to their home in the Capricornus constellation with the essential minerals and missing element their planet required.

Dharma opened her eyes and lifted her head off Lynx's shoulder, regaining consciousness just in time to see the train of gold and the Anunnaki disappear. 'Look!' she said pointing towards a hazy figure in the distance. 'Maria.' The lady stood in the light where the train had been, and then faded from sight.

'Can you walk? You weigh a ton, Dharms! Ouch!'

'Thank you,' She said, steadying herself.

'Wait, what did you just say?' The ground beneath them shook. 'See!'

'Funny! Let's get out of here.'

The agents sped through the collapsing Antarctic base, the caving ceiling destabilised the ornate arches, which shook the foundations of the ancient pillars. The pyramid base was crumbling like chalk.

'Drones!' Lynx aimed, ready to lock down the onslaught of pentagon pests.

'Timber …' Phoenix alerted. An enormous fallen pillar crashed to the ground, successfully taking out the approaching drones.

'Keep going; the entire base is coming down.' Dharma shouted, speeding through the great hall toward the chamber-way. 'Chamber-way's caving in,' she called, gaining a remote visual of the heavily obstructed passage-way. They clambered and climbed through the collapsing chamber-way.

'Argh, not cool.' Phoenix groaned, a crushing boulder landing on his leg. He whistled on the unit, immobilised and unable to move the rock himself.

'Oh mate, that's messed up,' Lynx said, squinting at the sight of Phoenix's crushed leg.

'You gonna carry me?' He said, laughing, then groaning under the pain.

'Got to get out of here, bud. The whole place is coming down.' Lynx signalled to Salva. They jacked the boulder and pulled Phoenix free.

'Don't think I can walk.'

'I've got you, bud,' Lynx said taking his weight through the crumbling chamber-way.

'Drones,' Dharma called. She and Salva opened fire at the swarm of micro-armed spies blocking the entrance back into the hangar. 'We've got this, take cover,' she shouted down the chamber-way.

The drone fire slowly stopped. Salva gently pushed the hangar door open, but by the time the door was fully open, thirty more strategic drones were on them. Dharma and Salva covered Lynx as he moved to take cover with Phoenix, resting him against a ripsaw. The Sarispa's metal warriors multiplied and appeared from every corner, floods of firing stuns lit the hangar and the Antarctic sky.

'Argggh son of a ...' Dharma grimaced. She didn't stop to check the wound, but fired ferociously, taking out the offending drone and all others within range.

'You hit?' Salva shouted to her, slowly turning, surreptitiously checking the calming hangar.

'Just a scratch,' she said, glancing at the bullet wound. As she looked up, she caught a reflection in a ripsaw, a fast-approaching drone, aiming its weaponry, ready to fire.

'Clear.' Salva called time on the last drone standing.

'That's a bit more than a scratch,' Salva said, checking Dharma's wound.

'It's fine,' she said, lifting her hand off the bleeding hole on her arm. 'Bullet went straight through.'

A hydroelectric din throttled into life. Dharma and Salva slowly moved out towards the armoured tank parked in the entrance.

'Lady Maria?' Dharma said, climbing into the tank. Popping her head back out seconds later, she said, 'It's Lady Maria.'

The all-white armoured machine moved out onto the Antarctic landscape. What lay behind was a paradoxical vision, the spaceship appeared to follow the tank, disappearing as it passed over the threshold of the base.

'We're towing the craft? Sick!' Phoenix said, craning to watch.

'It seemed fruitless to let the craft destroy with the base,' Lady Maria said, shouting over the din. 'As I recall it, the ship's Captain is a Federation agent, so technically I'm simply returning long-overdue borrowed goods.'

'That's a Federation ship?' Phoenix enthused, then grimaced under the pain in his leg.

'Try not to move your leg, my love,' Maria said, looking over at Phoenix. 'You would need to ask the craft's Captain about the ship's heritage,' Maria said with a passing twinkle in her eyes. 'My loves, we really should stop the bleeding.'

The entirety of Dharma's left sleeve and Phoenix's trouser leg were red, a particularly gruesome sight, in stark contrast with their white flight suits. Feeling light-headed and disorientated, both Dharma and Phoenix barely held on to consciousness.

Salva acted. He grabbed the first aid kit, cut into the shoulder seam of Dharma's sodden suit and ripped the sleeve clean off, then cleaned and dressed the wound. 'That should hold till you see a healer,' he said, moving on to Phoenix. 'Patch you up, bud? Oh, that's rough.'

'Nix, is that your bone?' Dharma said, squinting through one eye.

'You need a healer,' Salva said, dressing the deep lesion as best he could in the tank.

'Thanks Salva, life saver.'

'I've spoken to Castra,' Maria shouted over the heavy mechanical overtones. 'He will rendezvous with you at your return coordinates.'

'Lady Maria, did you say Castra is at the rendezvous point?' Dharma asked, not sure she heard correctly.

'I believe so. We are approaching the coordinates, so we'll see.'

The horizon had busied on up: two spaceships, a tank and a commune of intergalactics gathered on the Antarctic landscape. The struggle to exit the tank was greater than the entering, especially for the wounded agents, but when they did Brodgar C.I.T. and Chiron, the Healer awaited them. The agents broke into spontaneous celebration, as much for the astounding sight of the craft being towed by the armoured tank driven by Maria, as the quantum banishment.

'OK, firstly, agents Alpha Bravo, secondly Lady Maria, thank you, thirdly, let's board and debrief in the safe zone. After you, Captain ...' Castra said, gesturing to Salva.

Chapter Twenty

The Moon Landing

Salva leaned into the ship and rested on its dark exterior. The organically intelligent spacecraft activated, the hatch reached down inviting the Captain and crew to board. The C.I.T. unit and Chiron the Healer entered the morphing spacecraft. Designed to meet the needs of the entering crew, the interior was a dome from home.

Castra took position at the central command station. Salva stood at the ship's helm, hesitating, glancing towards Castra. The Commander saluted the ship's Captain, and Salva took to his station.

Phoenix, a little disoriented, seemed confused as to where to sit.

'Perhaps this one?' Chiron suggested, guiding Phoenix to a wing pilot station. 'I'll patch you up when we reach the safe zone.'

Phoenix turned to look at Castra, who was watching the wounded agent with pride and gave him a thumbs-up. The third and final position on the bridge called upon Herc. A familiarity came to the ground control agent. He looked to Salva and Phoenix, then at Castra. The Commander's thumb was already held in the air. The newly formed flight crew engaged, entirely absorbed by the quantum-algorithmic spaceship.

'Good to see you back in action, Chiron. How's Rose holding up?'

'She's doing grand, Lynx. The healers will have her back in Brodgar before you know it.'

'Welcome aboard Lou, comfortably seated?' Leo entertained Dorada and Leda with a dramatized flight presentation. 'Then let's commence your safety demonstration ...'

'You buckled up back there?' Salva said, checking in on his wingmen. 'She's a quantum-algorithmic coaction controlled craft, and one of the best ever created. She works on an intuitive quantum level. Just relax, place your hand in the palm mould. She'll download to you directly.'

Neither Phoenix nor Herc knew exactly what a quantum-algorithmic coaction controlled ship was, but with their hands already resting in the morphing palm moulds, they were good to find out.

Salva placed his hand into the palm connector. An aurora of light awakened, the borealis began, and the spacecraft seamlessly took to flight. The interior visors lowered to display a panoramic view of space. Each of the intergalactics sat quietly, engaged in their own stories being told in the stars. Almost instantly, and too quick for those lost in their celestial narrative, Lou transported the crew to the outer atmosphere of the Orion constellation.

Greeted by the glow of Betelgeuse, a sun and sustainer of life for the constellation, the rustic rays soon turned pink as the craft approached the Orion Nebula and anchored in the Federation safe zone. The crew activated. Chiron and Lynx helped Phoenix to the healing bay; moments later, the young agent left the room with his gaping wound healed. Dharma returned soon after, minus the drone shot wound and pain-free.

'OK. We have some solid intel and some projected incoming stats.' Castra said, standing at the central command station. 'We can confirm two out of the three scientists have been successfully passed through the quantum gateway. Simon Hedge and Beckett Normandy will infinitely be unable to enter this reality of Earth. However …' Castra said glancing down at the screen. 'The Council of Twelve have verified that Phinehas Coatl has returned to the matrix. As of now, we have no intel on her reboot, but it does look like Earth is already in the process of regenerating; storms and tectonic disturbance are balancing out. The data is still incoming, but stats are showing an encouraging shift. Well done everyone, good work.' Castra paused for a moment before continuing. 'Also confirmed,' he hesitated, 'is the creation ... of a parallel reality birthed by the Sarispa Collider.'

'Dirty little ...'

'Exactly, Leo. An act that would of course ensure the continued existence of the Sarispa within the multiverse. The Sarispa-created parallel Earth star system is a Federation priority. The Council believe within the system is an alternate Sarispa Thirteen, and a hundred and thirty-three thousand Sarispa.' The craft fell silent, yet the intel reached the agents in a place of knowing. 'To ensure the safety of the multiverse, the Federation requests the alternate Thirteen to be placed under immediate quantum lockdown.' He looked at his agents; their distinctly deflated expressions said it all. 'The good news is,' Castra continued, 'the Federation have passed the scientists to another unit. The Council have requested, in light of recent developments, developments meaning the craft, that Lou host and transport the mission unit's to Earth-Delta. Mission agents have been deployed to Orion's moon; units are awaiting transportation. Salva, the coordinates are en route for the Orion pickup point.'

'Received.' Salva's screen lit and the craft absorbed the intel.

Lou was a rare and valuable mode of intergalactic multidimensional transportation, created on Earth and built in South Africa by the Sarispa. The ship has the capacity to travel through time and space, and displace through quantum realms. Ships like Lou within this multiverse, were now more lore and legend than reality.

'When you're ready, Captain.' Castra said, sitting down at his station, preparing for flight.

'Stations secure?' Salva called out to the craft.

'Secure.'

The ship's pilots placed their palms into the organic moulds. A supernova of light merged; a fusion of intergalactic being and quantum-intuitive craft navigated through space.

Violet rays from the dust clouds graduated into darkness, and through the starlit galactic sky two orbicular auras appeared on the horizon. Lou sailed towards Mizan, a Federation-inhabited satellite orbiting the home of eighteen billion Orions. Eighteen billion beings that marvel and dream about life beyond Orion. The craft approached the dark side of the moon and prepared to land in the light of an illuminating stone circle.

Castra spotted Ashtar through the opening hatch and flood of amber light. The physical forms of the intergalactic beings appeared altered, their bodies harmonized to the shift in frequency. The unit watched from the ship the interaction between Castra and Ashtar. Castra appeared stouter than usual, and Ashtar also showed signs of a less elongated stature. During the exchange, Castra turned to look at the craft, tilted his head to one side, then gazed across the landscape. Through a sea of terracotta domes, the four-four-four mission agents walked towards the spacecraft.

'The agents are ready to board when you are, Castra,' Ashtar said, motioning the mission forward.

'Let's take it one unit at a time.' Castra said, his spatial awareness heightened, his faith that they would all comfortably fit on-board tested. 'One unit at a time. Next, that's it, keep it going.'

Castra followed the final boarding unit onto the ship, his hope that Lou would organically contract to meet the needs of the expanded crew exceeded his expectation. The craft morphed to its mission. 'Welcome aboard Lou,' he called from his command station, now an elevated spherical plinth in the centre of the evolving craft. Row upon row of occupied stations fell out before him, still in the final stages of transformation, the ship appeared to interact with the incoming energies, perhaps in celebration of the grand reunion. 'OK, just a quick briefing before we take off.' Castra said engaging the agents. 'Mission agents, you have successfully placed ten masters of the Sarispa Thirteen through the quantum gateway, Hitch being the only remaining Thirteen existing within this reality of Earth. Elflock and Coatl have both returned to the matrix, and with no confirmed intel, we can assume both will reboot at an opportune time. Our focus and mission for the time being is Earth-Delta, the Sarispa-created parallel Earth system. The Federation requires mission units to pass the Earth-Delta Thirteen through the quantum gateway.'

The news of Delta was new to many of the boarding agents, an unexpected twist in the mission and not altogether welcomed. Deadly and dark within a parallel manipulated to progress their own advancement, the agents could only imagine what they could be up against in a reality created by the Thirteen, for the Thirteen.

'Agents, time is of the essence. The Federation requires our immediate deployment.' Maps rolled out on the agents' screens. 'The location may look familiar: we are scheduled to travel to Teotihuacan Earth-Delta, exactly two weeks before the original Sarispa Scatterings. Commanders,' he called over the agents' increasing unrest upon learning the destination of the approaching deployment. 'We require ground crew to stay behind onboard, four agents from each unit.' The C.I.T. commanding officers assigned ground control agents to stay onboard. Castra called on Herc, Dorada, Leda and Rigel to take ground support for Brodgar.

'Salva, as the craft's Captain, you'll also remain onboard, do you have anything to add?'

'Thank you, Commander,' Salva said, standing to address the mission agents. 'We'll be travelling beyond our normal quantum travel experience today. Most of the journey will feel and seem similar to standard quantum travel, but as our displacement is not only back in time, but also to a parallel universe, I'll take you through a reminder of key travel stages. A bright light will appear at the end of the quantum passage; the craft will reach the point of light, beyond the speed of light. It may feel and seem like you're falling through a black hole. Don't panic, it's perfectly normal and actually instantaneous, although it might not feel so. Through the crossover, we will be outwith time and space; relative time within the void is, of course, nonexistent. The most comfortable way to pass through it is to simply close your eyes and transcend. The mind will want to create a reality or a sense of reality in any given situation, but the void has no reality; it's basically an empty chamber-way connecting one multiverse to another. The more tuned into the experience you are, the more prolonged and intense the quantum leap will be. So, when we reach the light, close your eyes and try to transcend beyond the travel experience.' Salva bowed and settled back into his flight chair.

'Thank you Captain. Agents, prepare for interdimensional flight.'

Chapter Twenty-One

Beyond Mandela

Salva's body vibrated in the turbulent transition; blinding light bore into him as the craft and Captain navigated beyond the speed of light to the point of the interdimensional leap. The void vacuumed the craft, rotated it 180° on its axis, then spat it out into an orbiting tunnel of darkness towards Teotihuacan, Earth-Delta. The entire crew, with the exception of one or two experienced interdimensional flight captains, were transparently affected by the extreme phenomena of the displacement; one quantum reality to another.

'Phoenix, the high-pitched screams?' Herc said, looking at Phoenix.

'To be honest, bud, they weren't that high. Am I right, Dharma?'

'You've been higher.'

'OK, OK,' Castra said, calming the crowd from the commander's platform. 'The craft will await returning agents within the present zone coordinates. The ship will remain in stealth mode, and I'm sure I don't need to remind you …' he said, staring out at his own agents in particular, 'that this is a covert mission!'

'Just a bit of the travel giggles, Castra,' Leo tried to say through his own spontaneous laughter.

'All units have been assigned to Masters of the Order,' Castra continued over the amused outbursts. 'However, should you encounter any of the Thirteen, assigned unit Alphas are to pass the Masters through the gateway. OK, questions?'

'Do we have a timescale we're working with, Castra?' Commander Tara of Stonehenge asked, projecting a soothing lilt throughout the craft.

'Thank you Tara, I'll pass you to Salva.'

'From the craft's point of view,' Salva said, standing to address the Arcturian Commander, 'I would estimate Lou has five, maybe six hours in a sedentary stealth mode before elemental metamorphosis sets in. It's an unknown universe …' Salva said, as his attention turned to the intel appearing on his screen. 'Lou concurs: five hours, six maximum.'

'OK, a four-hour turnaround,' Castra called it. 'Regardless of the outcome, return to the ship within four hours. Any other questions?' Castra glanced around the craft. The deploying agents were already standing, ready to head out.

Intense heat blasted through the lowering hatch. The field agents deployed, adjusting their travel-tempered eyes to the blinding Mexican light, leaving the sanctuary of Lou behind. Castra led the Brodgar agents towards the northern border of the fierce fortress peaked by three flat-topped pyramids.

'Blend and scale,' Castra told the field agents as they reached the citadel wall. Colours and textures merged; the agents and the fortress became indistinguishable. The unit shot upwards twenty metres from the ground, then scaled their way to the top of the Sarispa stronghold.

'Piramide de la Luna,' Castra said, greeting the looming pyramid as he reached the top of the fortress. His words were drowned out by raw sounds of the Sarispa settlement.

The Pyramid gave the city a clandestine cover. The agents' view of Teotihuacan was limited. Castra closed his eyes and scanned the area. 'We'll enter the city through the subterranean chamber-ways on the eastern side of the pyramid, through the bowels of the base towards the Pyramid of the Sun, and Hitch, be vigilant—the area could be heavily guarded. Descend.'

The ancient Mesoamerican metropolis felt barbaric; as soon as the agents landed on Sarispa soil they could feel the latent savagery. The unit manoeuvred in close proximity to the city wall, maintaining their blend, providing a covert arrival to the eastern entrance of the pyramid. The unit followed Castra down a narrow, steep declining chamber-way into the pit of the city. The stench of deep, dark death consumed the air; Leo in particular struggled with the repugnant reek. Castra spun in the tight space, attempting to locate the culprit of the retching sounds echoing through the chamber-way.

'I can't help it, Castra,' Leo said, talking through the cover of his hand, 'the place gives me the boke.'

'It is a bit stinkin.' Nash agreed, his hand over his mouth.

'The stench of death!' Lynx threw into the mix, and mix it did. Leo's boke was no longer dry, but wet and all up the walls. Ignoring Leo's inability to stomach the smell of the Sarispa chamber-ways, Castra ordered the unit to move out.

'Has he always been this harsh?'

Castra ignored Leo and led the agents down the chamber-way to the entrance of the base. The unit halted, hearing approaching footsteps draw close.

'Stonehenge unit,' Dharma reported, doing a rapid scan.

'We could hide and jump out on them?' Leo said through his hand.

'Right, that's it ...'

'Kidding! But seriously, Castra, you've got to loosen up. My guts are still churning from being sucked backwards through a black hole.'

'Loosen up? Let me tell you about loosening up ...'

'Sir,' Dharma interrupted.

'The Thirteen in four hours, a hundred and thirty-three thousand Sarispa in a twenty kilometre radius ...'

'SIR,' Dharma shot at the Commander again. Castra slowly, knowingly turned and looked behind.

'Castra, is everything OK?' Commander Tara asked, Stonehenge C.I.T. standing behind her listening and waiting for the Brodgar unit to cast their domestic issues to one side.

'Apologies, Tara,' Castra said, allowing the infamous unit to pass. 'Who are you shutting down?'

'Elflock. On our way there now.' Tara called and ran out of sight.

'See,' Castra said once the Stonehenge agents were out of earshot. 'They're nearly at Elflock's quarters, and we're stood here arguing.'

'Technically,' Dharma said, 'I'm still field unit Alpha?'

Castra looked around at the unit. His intuition fought back his ego; with the slightest dip of his head, Dharma assumed her position as unit Alpha.

'Move out,' she called.

The underground journey across the city towards Hitch's quarters became more harmonious and speedier. Leo's vomiting eased; he was sick only once more, shared this time with an audience of Bosnian C.I.T. agents, who appeared to be amused if not a little bilious. The sub chamber-ways of the Sarispa's parallel megalopolitan were encouragingly void of Sarispa. They passed a number of C.I.T. units, none of them quite as telling as their encounter with Stonehenge C.I.T. At one point, a drunk Sarispa guard staggered past the unit; the agents took to the ceiling and blended, but there was really no need.

'Oh my stars, let me through,' Leo called, his voice echoing through the transforming harmonics. He pushed through the unit, sensing the potential of free-flowing air, and with a burst of raw energy, Leo's swift power-walk broke into a gentle jog up the steep incline, reaching terra level just behind Dharma.

'It's swarming out there, and they're unsettled,' Dharma reported, pulling back from the concealed opening. 'Hitch's quarters are on the southwestern side of the Pyramid of the Sun, we're on the east side.' She took another scan of the immediate area. 'Security is too tight for a terra-level approach, and it's all their own first-generation lizards, no other visible intergalactics in sight,' Dharma said and started to walk back down the chamber-way. 'We passed a ceiling bay door about five hundred metres back.' She closed her eyes and scanned the downloaded maps. 'It should take us inside the pyramid sub-tunnels, which should ...' she paused to scan again, 'lead us directly to a concealed entrance and into Hitch's quarters.'

The senior agents gulped mouthfuls of air before setting off back through the grim subterranean tunnel. The unit approached the ceiling bay door. Dharma sent up a stun, the door released from the lock, and one by one the agents shot upwards into the cramped chamber-way.

'Expect the worst from the guard,' Dharma said, bringing the unit together before storming Hitch's Mesoamerican abode. 'These guys are the undiluted real deal, before galactic blending was even a thing. Dark and deadly. Make sure you've got everyone's backs, they like to hit from behind.'

'Chill, we know the evil wee dude is pumped, can we just do it?'

Dharma looked at Leo, then the unit; of course they knew. 'Move out.'

The agents sped down the chamber-way towards the entrance to Hitch's chamber. Dharma saw it, but before words could leave her mouth or protective actions be taken, her vision became her reality. A black explosion, motion slowed, she fell to the ground. Sarispa stuns shot through the solid obsidian door, knocking the entire unit out. The Brodgar agents lay covered in a mound of black dust. Hitch was ready and the guard was heavy. The unit didn't stand a chance.

'Bring the Arcturian female here and take the leftovers to the sacrifice chamber,' a dark reptilian humanoid ordered, studying its prey.

A black shadow flew out from the humanoid and encircled Dharma inconsequentially of its master, fervently moving around the unknown quantity, experiencing an unusual sensation. Hitch's shadow demon felt its own fear for the first time.

'Take her to the oracle chamber.' Hitch ordered, and two guards dragged Dharma out of the chamber. 'Open the armoury. Sell weapons, spread the word of war; tell it to the citadel, tell them an army has invaded our great Sarispa city.' Hitch snarled, filled with warmongering and moneymaking. 'Order them to hide their children; tell them the invaders wish to take them as their slaves. Release arms, set fires and raise the prices. Double the price of their defence. Destroy their lives, we may sell it back to them.'

Hitch selected six guards and sent the rest into the city to spread the word of war. Invigorated, the leader of the Thirteen turned his attention to the remaining Sarispa guards. 'You three,' he said, pointing to three unfortunate guards, 'protect my personal chamber vault. If the city is lost, remain at the vault; if you're dying, remain at the vault; if he is dead, remain at the vault.' His eyes, no longer humanoid but distinctly reptilian, spun in his head. He laughed a high-pitched laugh, sending his shadow demon into a torrent, shrouding the guards in a warning wave of darkness and terror towards his personal vault.

'Arcturian!' Hitch called out, leaving one chamber for another. 'Let us see what you can see.' Hitch, the shadow demon, and remaining

Sarispa guards marched through the chamberways, readied for war and heading towards Dharma.

Chapter Twenty-Two

Answered Call

'Unit down, repeat, unit down. Brodgar C.I.T. is out of the game.'

'The full unit, Herc?' Salva shouted over the orchestra of rising sound onboard Lou. 'Are they all together?'

'Full unit, except Dharma.'

'Where's Dharma?'

'The Pyramid of the Sun. By the looks of the surrounding biochemical reading I'd say she's being held in an oracle chamber,' Herc said, turning to look at Salva. The Captain was already halfway across the ship. Herc locked down the craft. 'I have orders from above.'

'What orders?'

'You are not to leave the ship under any circumstance, no exceptions. Sorry, bud.'

Salva ignored Herc and continued to override the hatch. He placed his hand in the scanner; the ship refused his request. He entered variants of numerical sequences; the craft refused the order.

'Herc!' Salva pleaded, 'They will kill her as soon as they download every memory, thought and vision she's ever had.'

Herc's eyes filled with compassion, but still, he returned to the ternaries.

Salva screamed at the hatch, punched it, kicked it; his emotive determination could not penetrate the craft's protective shields. A light from the helm and a muttering in his mind brought Salva back from the brink.

The Council of Twelve.

'Dharma,' Salva muttered and took up position at his station. 'Agents, prepare for interdimensional flight.' He placed his hand, fuelled and impassioned into the mould, and travelled to our reality of Earth. Anchored at

Teotihuacan, the Captain sent out a call to The Council of Twelve.

Hundreds of tourists baked in the midday Mexican sun, basked in the settlements' geopathic omissions, looking on in awe at the mysterious pyramid complex, entirely unaware of the intergalactic presence. Salva became restless. His hand motioned, readied to retreat, only too aware of the hundreds of agents on Delta relying on the craft's salvation.

'Captain.'

Twelve apparitions became solid form onboard Lou. The call was answered and the craft morphed to house the peacekeepers of the multiverse.

'I believe, Commander,' Salva said, looking directly at Ashtar, struck by the presence of the other eleven members, 'Dharma sent out a call to the Council.'

Ashtar thanked Salva for transporting the craft to Earth. 'But really, there was no need,' he said. 'The Council can displace almost anywhere instantaneously. We arrived on Delta looking for Lou.'

The craft continued to expand. Above the central command station a platform appeared, supporting an emerging round table large enough to seat twelve. The present serving Council was made up of four female members, Kuan, Vesta, Lady Maria and Lady Victorya. Four male members, Masiix, Hermex, Helios and Commander Ashtar, and four nonbinary beings, Kumara, Shani, Tusita and Loka, glided up a spiral staircase to the newly created Council station. Ashtar settled in between Lady Victorya and a hooded member of the Council, Hermex. The Federation Council prepared for interdimensional flight. With Dharma's call still echoing in his mind, Salva set course for Delta.

Chapter Twenty-Three

La Calzada de los Muertos. The Avenue of the Dead

Stunned in the depths of a sunken sacrifice pit, knocked out by a constant wave of dark light. The Brodgar agents would regain consciousness and motion; as they did, the circling guards would take them straight back out of action again.

Leo had had enough. The last stun wore off, he slung himself up onto his knees, arms waving in the air. The guards aimed their fire at Leo, offering a split-second opening for the C.I.T. agents to lock down the firing Sarispa.

'Get me the hell out of here,' Leo said, pushing Sarispa guards off him. 'Don't ever let it be said I won't take one for the team,' he grumbled, clambering out the pit, aided by Nash and Castra.

The rumblings of war filled the chamber-ways. The agents moved out and headed towards the Pyramid of the Moon's main hall. The space was filled with an eerie silence. On Earth, Sarispa darkness is held within this place, mystically amplified by the pyramid. It yields an intergalactic energy not akin to Earth or Earth-Delta's natural harmonics. The magnified energy had already begun to manipulate Delta's vibration. The intergalactic invaders emitted a frequency that was harmonically connected to their home planets of Rastaban and Eltanin. The occupation of the harsh nonterrestrial energies shrouded the place and the planet in an unsettling frequency. As living breathing organisms, Earth and Delta have to adapt to the shift the Sarispa brought with them.

The unit approached the pyramid's exit; the overwhelming sounds of the war penetrated their senses. They took a blended look out onto the city, where thousands of Sarispa guards lined the Avenue of the Dead—La Calzada de los Muertos. Thousands more marched through the city, terrorizing their own people. Alarms sounded, sirens soared; the city's occupants, queued to purchase weapons, ran to the safety of their homes and searched for missing children, fearing the so-called evil invaders had already captured and enslaved them.

'It's not looking good,' Castra said, pulling back into the cover of the pyramid, 'best and probably only option is to go back through the sub chamber-ways and head under the city again.'

'Where do you think he's holding her?' Lynx asked over the building orchestra of terror and trauma.

'Pyramid of the Sun probably, he'll want to keep her close.'

'Salva!' Leo piped up, completely sure he wasn't heading back into Teotihuacan's subterranean tunnels. 'The ship?' The unit looked at him. Their expressions all led to the same conclusion: of course Salva, of course the ship.

The hatch lowered. The agents halted, startled by the addition of the conference platform and the Council of Twelve; the morphed ship and the prodigious gathering gave just cause for their double-take.

'The city is sighted for war,' Castra announced to the elevated Council, 'units are unable to navigate across the city.' He acknowledged the imperial crew and headed to the helm. 'How's she doing?'

'Holding on in there; she's conscious for now.' Salva said, studying Dharma's code.

'What's her location?'

'The Pyramid of the Sun's oracle chamber.'

The intel of Dharma's whereabouts was not unexpected. Each of them had suspected if the Sarispa were ever to capture her, an oracle chamber would be her first port of call. The Arcturian's ability allowed her to transcend beyond her dimensional existence, her ability to see and know. Dharma could see and knew the multiverse's deepest, oldest secrets. Her secret was every secret. Hitch saw it and knew it the moment she entered his city.

'She's losing consciousness,' Salva urged.

'Lord Hitch has no intention of killing Dharma, not yet,' Ashtar said, taking to his feet, 'but true to his legacy, his actions are indeed dark and cruel. Hitch will attempt to break her down so that he may walk within her dreams. Agents, we must prohibit this action at all costs. In the wrong hands, the intel Dharma holds could bring devastating effects to the multiverse.'

'Commander,' Leo bowed, 'hell will become a luxury ski retreat before that happens.'

'I am extremely happy to hear that, Leo.'

'Hurry, she's fading,' Salva called out to the deploying unit.

'Units are in close pursuit of Elflock,' Herc called as the ship's hatch closed behind the Brodgar agents. 'A gateway's opening, but the agents have heavy company on the way.'

The Council of Twelve rose. A ring of interlocking energy surrounded the field agents; the pursuing Sarispa guard fell.

'It's done,' Herc called over the ship's rapid running commentary. 'Elflock has been passed through the quantum gateway. Three of the Delta Thirteen still stand: Coatl, Portland and Hitch.'

'Locations and units in pursuit?' Ashtar asked from the council platform, floating as if it were a Pleroma; a celestial base looking down on Earth.

'Coatl's located in the Quetzalcoatl temple, five units in pursuit; Callananish and Castlerigg are entering the temple; Nabta, Merry Maidens and Drombeg are en route, ETA ninety seconds.'

'Portland's location?'

'The Pyramid of the Moon. Six hundred Sarispa guards are surrounding his coordinates, attending C.I.T. units are Carrowkeel, Shasta, Knowth, Sedona, Iona and Kailash, additional units are en route. Units pursuing Portland are outnumbered and overpowered.'

The Council rose and the load lightened for the field agents. Portland's six hundred protective guards fell to three hundred.

'Hitch?'

'Heading towards Dharma's coordinates, thirty Sarispa guards at the oracle's chamber, three en route with Hitch.'

'Brodgar's ETA?'

'Four minutes.'

'Request all available units to attend the oracle chamber.' Ashtar said and placed a sound globe around the platform. Those present in the harmonic globe heard all sounds audible within the craft. Communication that took place inside the globe stayed in the globe.

'Lady Victorya,' Ashtar requested, proportional unease prompting his proposal, 'perhaps we should prepare for unforeseen likelihoods.'

Lady Victorya rose out of her chair, raised the hood of her blue sapphire cloak and watched; through the window of her mind's eye, she saw Dharma.

Chapter Twenty-Four

Salvador

A dark chamber emitted intoxicating fumes from a deep crevice in the earth towards the chamber's solitary occupant. Secured on a three-legged stool, Dharma slipped in and out of consciousness, reaching a cognitive state just long enough to sense the chamber was empty. The Sarispa stood guard on the other side of the door safe from their own mephitic manipulation.

The gases were entirely alien to Dharma; she wouldn't have long before they would transport her to an unknown realm. Approaching incapacitation and almost completely blind, her hands fell toward the crevice. Dharma's normally naturally induced light lay blank. Her mind became a collage of movies running a hundred to none; she slowed down the visions and picked one.

As if she were a bird, she flew over her lands, above the oceans, absorbing the vibrance and vibration of Arcturus. Rich rustic landscapes, pink and golden seascapes were flourishing with all manner of life. Her orbit let go and a solitary tear fell down her face. The light in Dharma's hands awakened. So very grateful for the lifeline, it grew, creating a shield over the gassy crevice.

Dharma returned halfway from the unknown and back again. She scanned the chamber-way; thirty guards at the entrance, three accompanying Hitch. Through the lifting haze, she sought backup. The closest units read as three minutes away. Her palms glowed in preparation as she watched Hitch approach the chamber.

The footsteps stopped. She lifted the shield covering the crevice and slumped into the stool. Hitch and his shadow skulked into the chamber, unaffected by the fumes. The master of the time and space and his demonic Archon companion stalked their prey.

'Supremely satisfying, I have to tell you, even in your …' he grabbed Dharma's hair and wrenched back her head, 'lesser state. Now let me see, which one are you?' Hitch lifted the lids of Dharma's eyes, 'well, aren't we the lucky ones, Lady ...' Hitch halted and looked up. Fresh footsteps approached the chamber-way. Crashing bodies hit the floor. The frenzied shadow-demon, unaccustomed to his master's tension, sent them both into a spin.

Like a sniper, from the side Dharma followed the demon's trail and sent out a stun. Disabled, the shadow-demon stumbled into its master's mind and tortured his narrative. Hitch fell to his knees to receive Dharma's stun.

'Who's the lucky one now, Hitch?' she said to his slumped body. A faltering light beamed from her palms; she shielded the gases and bequeathed her being to the opening quantum gateway.

The battle in the chamber-way reached the oracle chamber door. The entrance exploded, footsteps approached. Dharma turned to see. Blinded, she had to trust. The owner of the footsteps guided Dharma and the gateway towards Hitch. With the will of both, the gateway opened and commenced its dimensional journey. Sarispa fire intensified. Sensing Hitch's impending exile, the guard opened rapid rounds. Dharma battled to direct the building gateway; even with the aid of another, the gateway faltered. Warmth surrounded her; in her mind's eye, a veil covered her.

It was a cloak, not a veil that shielded Dharma from the onslaught of stuns. The gateway regained momentum, transcending towards its quantum destination, reaching the interdimensional prison with Hitch locked in. Lord Hitch and his shadow-demon passed out of existence. Engulfed by the experience, knocked backed by the quantum explosion, Dharma fell into the arms of the unseen intergalactic.

'He was not a lord or a leader for my people.' The stranger said, lifting Dharma off the stool.

'Salva?' Lynx questioned, rooted in the doorway with the Brodgar unit.

'Salvador.' The Sarispa guard bowed. 'You know my name?'

'Well you're …' Leo stammered.

'Sarispa.' Castra pushed past the C.I.T. agents. 'We've got to get her out of here.'

'Salva's Sarispa?' Phoenix said, rooted to the spot.

'This way.' Salvador urged the unit to move out. The chamber-way was clear for now, but news of Hitch's gateway would travel like wildfire through a forest of kindling. 'Down here,' Salvador called, opening a floor shaft, pulling it shut just as an approaching army of guards turned down into the chamber-way.

'Castra, did you know all this time?' Leo whispered.

The Commander nodded his head in response.

'Dharma knew; she for sure knew something wasn't right,' Phoenix said, quietly pulling himself into the exchange.

'Just leave it,' Castra shot at Leo and Phoenix.

'It's left for now, Castra,' Leo retorted.

Salvador led the agents deep into the depths of Delta; a thin veil blew in the wind between Hitch's personal escape route and Delta's Hollow Kingdom. At the end of the declining passage, Salvador cleared dirt from underfoot and revealed another hidden hatch in the floor. The Sarispa guard guided the unit through the empty escape chamber, devoid of all except an enormous vault and a concealed entrance.

'The door will lead you beyond the citadel,' Salvador said, resting Dharma into Castra's arms.

An uneasy silence fell throughout the unit. So many things they wanted to say to the Sarispa guard, yet they all stood in silence. Salvador waved and pointed again to the concealed doorway and set back off towards to the city.

Chapter Twenty-Five

A Karmic Return

A hidden hatch creaked open. Salvador checked the coast was clear, climbed out and set back towards the oracle chamber.

'Freeze! Piccola San Bernardo C.I.T.!' A young female C.I.T. agent, still a bit out of it, shot her hands in the air, ready to fire.

'Don't fire! I'll help you get out of the city. I helped your friends Castra and Dharma.'

'Castra and Dharma? Are you not the craft's Captain?' The confused intergalactic asked, rousing the semi-conscious agents lying around her.

'Quickly, I will lead you beyond the city.' Salvador guided the injured Federation agents from the oracle chamber to beyond the citadel, and then headed back out into the city.

'Where have you been?' A suspicious Sarispa guard questioned when he reached La Calzada de los Muertos.

'I was stunned.' Salvador muttered and moved beyond the inquisitive guard.

'Where is Lord Hitch?' The guard shouted after him. He ignored his protests to come back and answer him and headed out into the street.

Thousands of leaderless Sarispa guards stood bewildered along La Calzada de los Muertos. Unsettlement spurred an uprising. They called his name, chanted for Hitch to appear, called out to Elflock, to Coatl, demanded Portland. None would come. None but one.

He walked through the city, through the guard and climbed the steps to the podium rooftop of the Pyramid of the Moon. Two hundred and forty-eight steps; the time in steps it would take a craft to travel from Rastaban to Earth. He reached the pinnacle of the pyramid and The Council of Twelve. He knew not why, what he would say or do, only that he should. The young Sarispa guard stood in the presence of the divine peacekeepers of the multiverse.

'Salvador!' Ashtar welcomed the Sarispa guard and activated a sonic amplifier. 'We greet and welcome you travellers from Eltanin and Rastaban.'

A wave of light washed through the city. Darkness was lifted on that day, lifted from the city and its interdimensional inhabitants. The Sarispa guards looked at one another, independent souls, minds, hearts and spirits set free. The Sarispa guard fell out, stood down, and, probably for the first time, were at ease. Townsfolk, men, women and children left the safety of their homes, no longer afraid, no longer terrorized or traumatized by the life to which the Sarispa Thirteen had held them hostage.

'You are sovereign souls, no longer held or bound by the laws or limitations placed on you by the Sarispa Thirteen,' Lady Victorya addressed the collective; her words chimed throughout the city. 'We The Council of Twelve decree that war, profiteering and destruction be forever forbidden on Delta.'

'Acts of violence and terrorism stand in direct violation of the intergalactic law that governs this planet,' Hermex of the Twelve spoke to the collective, wearing a camel cloak with a peaked hood that did not fully disclose his identity.

'Sarispa of Earth-Delta, you are free to leave the city or indeed to remain at Teotihuacan.' Masiix, longhaired and bearded, presented the Sarispa guard to the city. 'Salvador has elected and been selected to bridge the gap between Delta and the Council, an open channel between the Intergalactic Federation and you.' Masiix turned to him and encouraged him to address the crowd.

'No matter who you are,' Salvador said, stepping out, his voice resounding throughout the city, 'no matter where you are from or what you have experienced,' he said, stepping closer to his people. 'You choose. The world we create, the life we live, the legacy we leave. The choice is ours.'

A solitary handclap built into a wall of sound.

'SALVADOR- SALVADOR- SALVADOR.'

The Sarispa guard raised his hands to quiet the chanting crowd. 'You do not need to chant my name. I will serve you, we will serve each another. We will evolve to bring peace, create to bring joy ...' The city ignored Salvador's protests and continued to chant his name anyway.

'Manipulation and modification will destabilise Delta; be kind to your planet,' Ashtar brought the proceedings to a close. 'Coexist naturally with your planet, harmoniously, and Earth-Delta will systemically regenerate, serve and sustain for many trillions of years.'

A golden auric glow adorned Ashtar and the peacekeepers of the multiverse. The Council of Twelve became an effervescent haze and disappeared from the Pyramid of the Moon, Earth-Delta.

It took days for the celebrations at Teotihuacan to eventually fizzle out. Their timely release from enslavement led many of the Sarispa to leave the city, never to return. The duplicated travellers from Rastaban and Eltanin began building settlements, at first mirroring those on their earthly counterpart, but soon enough the clever intergalactics grew beyond the boundaries and teachings of the Thirteen. They connected to the planet, heard its song and followed its lines. Eventually, peacefully settling throughout the

Sarispa-created planet, their planet, set in a parallel reality to our planet, the home they had lost through war and destruction, came back tenfold.

Chapter Twenty-Six

Mysteries Revealed

Dharma drifted in and out of consciousness, slipping between realms and dimensions. She was eventually aroused by loud whispering beside her bed. She lay still and in darkness, but happy to be waking up, listening to her friends.

'She moved,' Leo said, leaning in towards her, 'don't try to open your eyes, lovey. Phoenix, go call a healer.'

'She's coming round!' Phoenix called, swinging the healing bay door open.

'Thank you, my dears,' the elder healer said, entering the bay. 'Can you hear me, my love?' Dharma motioned to speak. 'That's OK,' the healer lifted a drink to her lips. 'Would you leave us for a few moments, I would like to check Dharma's eyes.'

'We'll be just outside if you need us,' Leo said, holding the door open for Lynx, Phoenix and Nash.

The healer gently lifted layers of organic matter from Dharma's eyes and examined the burns from the oracle chamber. The bay door opened again. Dharma lay drowsy, but with the absence of eye dressings, she was happy to almost see her unit.

'You had us worried, girl,' Leo said, clasping her hand.

'What did I miss?' she rasped.

'What did you miss? Well girl,' Leo said, ready to enter into a full-action replay.

'My loves, Dharma needs to rest. Come back later.'

'When later?' Phoenix asked, waving goodbye. Dharma had already fallen back into sleep.

'A short visit this evening should be fine.'

'She'll be as good as new, she's tough,' Leo assured the agents walking along the beach, comforting himself as much as the others. 'Anyone hungry?' he asked, approaching the café.

'Starving, obviously. Need a hand?' Phoenix asked sitting at a table at the water's edge.

'Just you take that load off, lovey,' Leo called, turning on the fairy lights. Nash turned up the music and together they cooked up a feast.

It felt like time had slowed down. They slumped into their post feast lull, having exhausted all conversations concerning anything and everything. They took to watching the water. It seemed to take twice as long for early evening to arrive, but finally it did, and they prepared to visit Dharma. The agents stood ready to head back along the beach to the healing bay when they spotted a woman walking along the beach. Sand in her feet, red hair blowing in the wind. A pebble levitated and skimmed across the water, then another, then ten more. The precisely positioned stones formed a heart, the interstellar energy conductor raised the heart high into the sky.

'Dharma!'

'Did the healers let you go?' Lynx asked, curious about her release.

'Not exactly.'

'Come on girl, you look starving.' Nash said, helping her settle down at the table.

'I am a bit hungry.'

'Have you spoken to Ashtar or Castra?' Lynx asked.

'Not seen either of them yet, I'm sure I'll be summoned soon enough.' Dharma said, looking out to sea, gathering her thoughts, trying to see what she could remember from Delta. She recalled a hazy image of Hitch passing through the gateway, but that was about it. 'I don't see or remember much,' she said, ushering someone, anyone, to give her a breakdown of the mission's missing puzzle pieces. No one appeared particularly forthcoming. 'Well?' she said.

'Well what?' Phoenix said looking at Lynx, avoiding Dharma's stare.

'Did we lock them all down?'

'Oh that, yeah.' Phoenix said, letting out a dismissive, nervous laugh. 'We sure did; all thirteen of them locked down and passed through the gateway. No more Sarispa Thirteen on Earth-Delta.'

'Delta done! Yip, all Thirteen of them done and dusted,' Lynx chimed in, wiping his hands.

'You're weird. Why are you both weird?' she asked, staring at them.

'You need to go speak to Ashtar and Castra,' Lynx said, but the look on his face only goaded her curiosity.

'I'm not going anywhere, just tell me what happened. Here's Leo. Leo what happened at Teotihuacan? Those two are being weird.'

'It was all a bit of a shock,' Leo said, laying out cutlery for Dharma. 'Maybe you should wait until tomorrow, until you feel a bit stronger, lovey.' They all knew from her expression that waiting until tomorrow was not going to happen. Leo took a seat. 'Do you remember anything about Hitch's lockdown?'

'I remember,' Dharma said looking into her mind's eye, seeing exactly what she could remember. 'I can see Hitch being placed through the gateway, I have some memories leading up to his chamber, I remember you puking.'

'Sensitive stomach. I'm happy to own it, but nothing else?' Leo asked. Her exasperated expression fuelled him forward. 'OK girl,' he took a deep breath. 'You had help.'

'Help? I did, with what?'

'And more than once. Hitch's lockdown, you had help.'

'I did?' she said, more confused than ever.

'Dharms, or perhaps we should say my Lady,' Leo was gone, he stretched across the table, grabbed her hand, tears rolling down his face.

'What!'

'OK, OK. So you were passing Hitch through the gateway, you remember that. We were outnumbered. The Sarispa guard broke through and opened fire on you.' Leo took a deep breath.

'And?'

'A blue sapphire cloak, Dharms!' Leo squealed, 'the cloak shielded you, it saved you, girl.'

Stunned into silence, she looked out to the water. The lore of the cloak is legendary amongst the Federation and beyond. Its appearance is rarely seen by the wearer and only ever worn by those that have elected and been selected to stand within The Council of Twelve.

'You're sure it wasn't a brown blanket?' She joked, still looking out to sea; somehow, it seemed instantly more infinite. 'What was the other help? You said I had help more than once.' The ensuing silence quickly became awkward. They shuffled in their seats, glancing at one another, seeing who would disclose the missing link.

'Salva!' Phoenix said, pointing across the beach.

'Looks like he has the weight of the world on his shoulders,' Dharma said, watching him walk towards them.

'Well about that, the thing is,' Leo said, 'the other help you had was from, well it was from ... Salva.'

'Salva? I thought he was ordered to stay onboard Lou.'

'He was, look I don't know how to say this, so I'm just gonna spit it out, girl. Salva saved your ass, our ass and a whole lot of other asses, too.'

'From the ship?' she asked, looking up to see where he was on his approach.

'No, not from the ship; he was already in the city when we arrived. Salva was part of Hitch's personal guard detail, except he didn't protect Hitch—he helped you, he helped you pass Hitch through the gateway.' Leo looked up. 'The cloak, Dharms, the cloak was around you both.'

Salva reached the table, feeling uneasy. The obvious silence upon his arrival did not bring any relief to his feelings.

'You're out of the healing bay. How are you, how's your eyes?' he asked, looking at the red markings around her eyes. Their inquisitive gaze lingered as he took a vacant seat next to Dharma.

'They'll be fine in a couple of days,' she said, not removing her curious stare from his.

'You hungry Salva? You must be starving, lovey,' Leo said, pulling Nash to his feet. 'We'll just clear these away.' Leo and Nash quickly cleared the table, ushering Lynx and Phoenix to help them. 'Many hands an' all that.'

'Listen,' Salva said as soon as the rest of the unit was out of earshot, 'what happened out on Delta, down in the city was news to me.'

'I really wish it was news to me,' she said.

'Right, where are you up to?'

'You saved me and lots of other agents, too; and the cloak, they were bursting to tell me about the cloak.'

'Ashtar and Castra have just finished briefing me, and yeah. the cloak is massive. Anyway, they said I helped, well parallel-me obviously, Salvador, helped the injured Feds escape the city.'

'So ... you are Sarispa?'

'I was, I am.' He looked to the ocean for the words.

'You don't need to explain Salva,' she said, leaning in, placing her hand on his.

'I want to, I really want to explain. I really do,' he said placing his hand on top of hers. 'Delta, visit her now, visit the Sarispa without Hitch, without the Thirteen. After the lockdown of the Thirteen, the Council declared Delta an autonomous planet and Salvador a mediator. The Sarispa are … man, they're advanced, technologically, ecologically, but you know, it's the way they're working with the planet, with

Delta. My people are beautiful people, you can see it on Delta. The power of the Thirteen overwhelmed them on Rastaban and Eltanin, overpowered them on Earth, but without the Thirteen on Delta, they live peaceful, productive, planet-friendly lives.'

'No war?'

'Nothing. Hitch incited and led virtually every war on Rastaban, Eltanin and Earth, and virtually always played both sides. Without Hitch or the Thirteen, Delta will exist in peace. When you control the stream of intel to your city or into your planet, you can tell your people just about anything.' Salva said, looking to the home he still mourned.

'I take it you travelled Delta's timeline?'

'I did.'

'Ashtar's happy?'

'Ashtar's happy.' He smiled at her. 'No matter where you are in the multiverse, there will always be those that function through fear; well maybe not all, probably not on Arcturus.'

'Maybe not on Arcturus; my people have evolved to peace, but I've have seen plenty

Arcturians on Earth that live in a whole lot of fear. Singular displacement is complicated. Mass forced displacement puts the planet at risk.'

'Without the dark dictatorship, the Sarispa are free to learn, to make mistakes, of course, but to learn from them. The goodness my race holds, you could see it, and you could feel it.' His pride for his people and his joy for their new home was clearly audible. 'To be able to see and experience my ancestors having a second chance, a first chance, it meant a lot.'

'Can I ask a question?'

'Sure.'

'How did you, you know, end up in the Federation?'

'The answer to that is long and complicated, but the portion that I think you're asking about, is by the sound of it, similar to the events that took place at Teotihuacan Delta, and definitely more than a bit mirrored. So, the Federation were sending in units to Teotihuacan to shut down the Thirteen, they had prior warning from the oracle at Delphi and escaped before the Federation arrived. The Thirteen fled the city and left us to destroy you.' The light in Salva faded; a dark place from a long time ago haunted his face. 'Dharma, the things they did to their own people, we were slaves to the rule of the Thirteen. We had no idea the destruction of Rastaban and Eltanin was down to them. We were fed and led by fear and manipulation. They created and held all the cards.'

'I know what they did to your people, Salva,' she said, reassuring him. The light in her eyes encouraged him to continue.

'Hitch had the matrix and the leys covered. The Federation agents were being taken down before they could even reach Teotihuacan, if they did make it as far as the city, they were stunned as soon as they did. The majority of the Feds were travelling through the Bermuda vortex. I was stationed to attack from Teotihuacan, but somehow, something inside of me knew, I just knew it was wrong. I left my post, headed to the Bermuda vortex and gave the Federation agents the heads-up. It didn't take long for the oracles to pass on the shift in activity to the Thirteen. Hitch obliterated the Bermuda vortex, and I never went back. The Federation took me in and put me through basic training.'

'I'm glad they did.'

The paradigm shift Salva created that day stood as a shield, a defensive wall against Hitch and the Thirteen. Neither Hitch or Salva ever knew it, but Salva's actions somehow stood in opposition against complete and total planetary domination.

'Can I ask another question?' she asked.

'You don't need to ask. I want you to know what you need to know.'

'Why keep it secret, why not be open?'

'The Federation wanted and willed for me to be open. Ashtar fully advised towards transcending transparency. I just couldn't. The time didn't feel right, I guess; maybe that's the Sarispa in me. It was just always more important for me to serve and continue to serve until alignments clicked and the right time presented itself. It wasn't that I didn't want to share, or that my purpose wasn't pure,' he smiled at her. 'You knew though, didn't you?' he said, relaxing a little into his chair.

'I knew everything wasn't quite as it was being told, or not being told.' she said, watching him watch her. 'I am sorry Salva, truly, for what you went through, for ...'

'Forget it,' he said, smiling and peaceful. 'You knew, I knew you knew, you have nothing to be sorry about. It's me that should apologise to you.'

'So,' she said changing the subject. 'I hear you're to be the first intergalactic of Sarispa descent on The Council of Twelve.'

'Yes, that is the word about town, and you, the Twelve?'

'Who knew?' she said, leaning in a little closer, looking beyond him. 'Looks like someone knew you were hungry.'

'Who knew,' Salva said, following her gaze to Leo and Nash, who were approaching with yet another small feast.

Chapter Twenty-Seven

Cenote Surprise

Surrounded by sound, the morning songbird and Dorada giving it large in the shower, the ground agent was chirpier than the early morning aviary.

'You'll be late for the briefing, Dharms,' Dorada called, closing the door to the roundhouse.

Reluctantly, the intergalactic climbed out of bed, stepped through the shower, pulled on her flight suit and headed to the C.I.T. dome. She met with Lynx and Phoenix. Together they followed the smell of coffee and muffins wafting through the air, enticing them to the early morning briefing.

'So, Dharms, are we thinking you're heading to The Council of Twelve, is that what we're thinking?' Phoenix asked, attempting to keep up with her long strides up the hillside.

'We think,' she said smiling at him, 'that you're sitting next to Dorada today.'

'No, but seriously, what's your thoughts?'

'My thoughts are,' she said, reaching the entrance to C.I.T., 'Leo and Nash have brought breakfast, coffee and muffins – now that I know.' She winked at him, swung open the door, grabbed breakfast and sat down at her station to read the latest ternary updates.

'Morning everyone,' Castra said, greeting the unit. 'OK, good job on Delta; now back to Earth.' He glanced up at the agents, making sure the unit was awake and following. They were all a little bleary but seemingly engaged. 'No intel on Elflock or Coatl's reboot, and Hitch is on the move. He left London at 3:00 a.m., travelled the matrix to Paris, left Paris at 3:30 a.m., then travelled to Frankfurt. At 4:45 a.m., he enters the matrix in Frankfurt, travels to Vienna then Naples, Tokyo, then onto New York. He's worried. Ternaries are showing an inspection of his subterranean vaults at each of his stops; a short briefing with each of his cartel commanders, then he's on the move again. Latest intelligence shows Hitch and ten thousand Sarispa guards exiting the matrix at Chichen Itza, Mexico.' Castra ignored the audible shift in reaction to Hitch's sizeable mobile army and continued to read through the accompanying notes. 'The Council have advised minimal use of the matrix but have granted mission units permission to travel to Brodgar.' Castra took to his feet, spoke quickly and quietly with Salva, then set off to welcome the arriving units.

The four-four-four mission agents had already begun to amass in the stone circle when Castra arrived at the henge; by the time he reached the centre of the ring, he was surrounded by a constant flow of intergalactic apparitions.

'That's some pool of mercury,' Dharma said, joining him through the sea of arriving agents. 'I take it we're watching for tectonic disturbance?' Dharma asked, sounding concerned by the appearance of the silver liquid amassing in the circle.

'They've been watching Hitch's silver trail through the night, shifting ten thousand Sarispa, Tokyo to New York, straight through the Pacific ring of fire is just asking for trouble,' Castra said, shaking his head. 'As you would expect, it's caused seriously heightened global seismic activity. Ashtar's got a dedicated team on it.'

'Yeah, I didn't think it was down to these guys travelling to Brodgar.' Dharma said looking skyward. Lou appeared on the horizon, glowing in the light of the rising sun.

The hatch opened and a phosphorescent tunnel of light transcended to Earth; multiples of four passed through the gravitational tunnel and entered the morphing spacecraft. Castra boarded last and took the central station. The hatch shut, and Salva brought the mission to flight.

In a momentary displacement, the craft and the four hundred and forty-four Federation mission agents arrived at Chichen Itza. From dawn to dusk, the Brodgar sunrise was almost instantly replaced by the Yucatan sunset.

The ancient Sarispa base was void of any and all visiting tourists. Salva circled the site and landed the craft on the edge of the settlement's surrounding forest. The ship blended and the crew looked out to El Castillo—the Castle—a looming stepped pyramid situated in the heart of the intergalactic settlement.

The deploying crew were met with a synchronistic, ceremonial light show. Two shadow serpents, one on either side of El Castillo's looming staircase, awakened. The ascending reptiles cast a darkness as they slithered up the stepped pyramid, sending a sacrificial flare to meet with the black moon rising; alerting Hitch, the games had begun.

Deep below El Castillo in a subterranean chamber, Hitch rolled his eyes in manic expression; the offering had arrived. 'Prepare the cenote for sacrifice,' he said, 'bring me the Sarispa traitors and the Arcturian female. Kill the rest.' The awaiting guard bowed and scuttled off through the dark chamber-ways. Turning to an awaiting cleric, Hitch ordered, 'Inform the confederates, prepare for ceremony; time has aligned.'

The Federation's arrival was expected, and the Sarispa were prepared. El Castillo flooded with swarms of Sarispa guards. The awaiting assault opened fire on the C.I.T. agents. Castra led mission agents into the pyramid after Hitch. The remaining defending agents held position on top of El Castillo, forming a tight ring around the perimeter of the pyramid. Tidal waves of light washed thousands of stunned Sarispa down the pyramid steps. The rules of war when dealing with a race that thrives on battle are simple: defend against them. The Federation defensively positioned themselves around the perimeter of the pyramid's four sets of steps. Ninety-one steps multiplied by four, with one more step signified in the rooftop temple, brings the total amount of steps on El Castillo to three hundred and sixty-five, built to bring Hitch a daily reminder to appease the Quetzalcoatl, and his own dark fear.

***

'Keep it moving,' Castra shouted down the line, pausing to bring up the rear.

Dharma and Salva led the units through the pyramid's sub chamber-ways, down towards El Castillo's inner pyramid. The pyramid within the pyramid.

'How many have we got on our tail?' Salva shouted over the building terra-level battle.

'Got to be a thousand or more to the rear; ahead, the base is a bogie,' she shouted back and sent out the telepathic message to any and all agents that could receive the non-verbal communication. *Sizeable ambush ahead, Bloods and*

Sarispa guard, numbers not clear. At the end of the chamber-way blend, hit and run the pyramid high.

Dharma and Salva turned to each other at the end of the chamber-way; sounds silenced, motion slowed, their energies conjoined. They aimed at the doorway, and the entrance to the base exploded. Together the Arcturian and the Sarispa generated a shield, a relentless wave of energy that held back the assault from thousands of Bloods and Sarispa guards. Shielded, the four-four-four unit stormed the pyramid and ran high along the angular walls.

'Castra ...' Dharma shouted, alerting the commander to the faltering shield.

'Units are in position,' he screamed back.

'Hitch is in the cenote, you ready to run?' she said to Salva.

'Call it.'

The shield fell, the barricade disappeared, and a blanket bomb of enraged stuns shot through. The energy battle began.

They ran high and fast. Salva caught her attention, pointing towards an ornamental serpent hook on the wall. They turned and looked at the outnumbered crusade behind them and continued on to pursue Hitch. Salva reached out as he ran, ready to awaken the secret serpent.

'Wait!' Dharma called, halting his motion. 'Castra.'

The Commander waded through the sea of stunned bodies, escaping the battle to join their quest.

Dharma and Salva aimed their palms at the entrance to the cenote. Salva reached for the serpent hook. His hand froze in motion.

Awaiting marksmen stunned the three from behind. The entrance to the cenote opened; Sarispa guards, robed and concealed, dragged the agents into the ceremonial cavern and cast them to the edge of the sacred cenote.

'Quetzalcoatl!' Hitch called skyward. Birds fled through the cavern, through the oculus in the ceiling, fleeing to safer climes. With the arrival of the sacrifice, the ceremony commenced. 'The mighty Thirteen have stumbled. Ten of our thirteen sacred bloodlines have been taken from us. I present to you ten exceptional candidates to stand within this most honoured position. Great

Quetzalcoatl, we ask of you this final call: the Thirteen must not fall.'

The lids of Dharma's eyes lifted. Through the narrow openings and stunned haze, she saw a mirage of Sarispa centred around the cenote, haunting ceremonial masks concealed the candidates' identity: a double-headed reptile, one representing Rastaban, the other Eltanin, and a pyramid with three golden number threes. As elaborate as it was, the embellished mask did not disguise the identity of the centric robed figure.

'Great Maligno of the sky and stars, we bring treasures, an Arcturian female and two Sarispa traitors.' Hitch, possessed by dark fear, called out to his god. 'Great Quetzalcoatl, we bring you the greatest of riches.' Hitch signalled to the guard. 'Bring them.'

Dharma stilled her breath. The masked guards dragged her, Salva and Castra to the cenote edge.

'Great Quetzalcoatl, take these treasures as gifts.' Hitch called out to the serpent in the sky. 'Unite the Thirteen.' His shrill rang through the subterranean cave, awakening a latent dark presence. He signalled to the guard. The C.I.T. agents fell deep into the sacrificial waters.

The congregated masked figures raised their hands skyward, chanted to their deity, and watched the Sarispa offerings until they could be seen no more. Ripples replaced the agents' sinking bodies as they fell into the dark depths of the sacrificial subterranean pool.

Hitch, crazed, sent a dark beam skyward. A black light and the blood of billions of beings flowed through him, through the oculus, through time and space, to the place that had once been home.

Freezing subterranean waters awakened their senses. Salva pointed downwards. Castra and Dharma followed his lead deeper into the cenote towards an emerging waterway. The smallest of air pockets gave life to the three.

'You two lockdown Hitch and stun the confederates; I'll build the gateway,' Dharma said, gasping in a deep inhale of breath from the air pocket. The agents took one last intake then swam to the centre of the cenote. Like aquatic bullets, they shot through the water, through the surface, rising high above Hitch and the masquerading intergalactics. Salva and Castra let out a barrage of stuns, and Dharma grew a bright white light. From her elevated levitating position, from the depths of her being to the palms of her hands, the Arcturian opened a quantum gateway.

'Thought you might need a hand!' Leo called, sending stuns from the entrance with the rest of the Brodgar unit.

An enormous white triangle engulfed Hitch and the gateway consumed the cavern. The leader of the Sarispa was frozen in time and locked in space. The transcending gateway commenced interdimensional growth, moving quickly through the seventh to the eighth dimension. Hitch's being fell from all earthly realms and realities; he slipped through the ninth to the tenth dimension. The hypersphere exploded, optical phenomena streamed from the gateway and the subterranean cenote lit like a rainbow pyramid. The doorway to the eleventh dimension opened.

Dharma's hovering form held the gateway and released Hitch into the quantum vacuum. The vortex transcended, the whirlpool turned black, and the dark interstellar light that desperately sought Eltanin and Rastaban vacuumed, through time and space, through the closing gateway.

So very dark were the losses, the actions and behaviours, that his entirety, his eternity was filled with fear. When the actions of one soul contribute to such deep insurmountable loss, the loss of Eltanin, the loss of Rastaban and the near loss of Earth when you attempt to disempower, control and mass manipulate through money, war and media, your existence will forever be the personification of fear itself. Gone was the dark shadow surrounding the planet, beyond all and any reality, the multiverse time and space. Hitch was a nebula in the night sky for all eternity.

The cavern shook. Mounds of earth and sheets of limestone fell from the oculus into the cenote.

'Dharma, get the hell out of there!' Salva screamed, attempting to awaken her from the quantum haze. The gateway faded and Dharma fell, plummeting back into the cenote with the sheets of fallen limestone.

'Move out!' Castra ordered the unit to go.

Salva ran to the cenote and prepared to dive in. A tidal wave washed him back from the water's edge. Dharma broke through the surface, flipped and landed on the bank of the collapsing cenote. 'Let's go …' she said, smiling at him as she ran past.

Salva glanced back at the collapsing ancient sacrificial space and ran. The Brodgar unit joined the dispersing melee, Sarispa and Federation agents all dropping arms, escaping the pursuing tsunami, falling out through the flooding pyramid, lifting as many stunned agents out onto terra level as they could carry.

The Sarispa and the Intergalactic Federation stood together on the grounds of the ancient Sarispa settlement, watching El Castillo sink into the ground. The subterranean cenote swamped and swallowed the place of darkness. In a world where darkness was no longer endured, the pyramid sank deep within the Earth.

Still, silent and speechless, the Sarispa watched the stronghold fall into the sinkhole. Leaderless, without cause or dictatorship, the ancient army of Sarispa stood paralysed.

'Gather the dead and wounded.' Castra ordered, 'Salva, bring Lou in.'

Salva moved through the sea of bodies surrounding the sunken pyramid. The Sarispa watched his every step, his every motion; he paused, sensing the formation. Slowly, he turned and faced the leaderless Sarispa.

'Gather your dead and wounded,' he told them.

The Sarispa dispersed and followed his guidance. The dawn of the new era filled the Sarispa not only with fear, but also with hope. They feared Salva, the Sarispa traitor, but the Federation Captain who stood before them brought hope. Life after Hitch had hope. Salva presented and represented the embodiment of that hope to the leaderless intergalactics.

The C.I.T. agents boarded Lou and took off. A moment's displacement later, Salva, Lou and the Brodgar unit arrived back at Chichen Itza. The Sarispa boarded the Federation craft and transported their sick and wounded to Serpents Mound. The journey from the intergalactic healing base to Brodgar brought a minute's silence to the crew, without time to digest or absorb the enormity of the mission. Lou landed back in the Ring of Brodgar. The unit disembarked to a celebrating walkway of welcoming islanders. Ashtar walked through the gathering to the front of the crowd.

'We have long foreseen the potential for this day, who would have thought it was today.'

'Your place or mine, Ashtar?' Leo shouted through the crowds and cheers.

'Yours, obviously.' Ashtar cheerfully called back and led the beings of Brodgar down the hillside towards the beach.

The C.I.T. agents, with the exception of Leo and Nash, congregated at the end of a long table. Dharma pulled her gaze from the ocean and looked at Salva from across the table.

'The first day we arrived for the four-four-four mission,' she said, 'how did you get to the briefing on time?'

'Matrix, same as you,' he said, reaching for the arriving food.

'How did you not get pulled into Ashtar's quarters?'

'I did right after you I passed you on the beach, did you think you were the only one to get pulled up?'

'I don't know, I never thought about it before now, but that will be why,' she said rolling her eyes as the missing puzzle piece slotted into place.

'What will be why?' Salva asked through a mouthful of Margherita pizza.

'Why we were the only two in the detail ordered to arrive via terrestrial methods.' Dharma said, dawning comprehension flooding her Arcturian features.

'The cloak,' Castra said, sitting down at the beachside table. 'Two Council of Twelve apprentices travelling the matrix at the same time as the Council would read as thirteen, cause a glitch and create a wormhole.'

'So, that's one mystery solved, onto the next,' she said, smiling at Castra, tentatively manoeuvring the conversation. 'The whole, you know, Sarispa traitor thing?' She knew Castra wasn't of Sarispa descent, but was still intrigued why Hitch had called him a Sarispa traitor.

'After the Scatterings, the Sarispa were in chaos; the Federation needed people on the inside. I wasn't the only one,' Castra said, looking toward Leo and Nash who were approaching with more plates of food.

'It's not a secret, just not something many of us want to recall. They were dark times, but not anymore, baby!' Leo said, raising a glass.

'Brodgar!' The intergalactic islanders rose to their feet.

Their collective gratitude was interrupted. The sky darkened, birds flocked and bats fled. The light left early and the chaos came in quick.

'Earth's sovereignty.' Ashtar boomed, and a force fired from his being.

The island's spherical domed phenomenon illuminated, and the intergalactic Federation watched from the Brodgar beach, as seventy-two lit triangles appear in the reality above the dome.

The matrix merged with the ancient dark beings, the last in a line until the end of time, and then there was light.

Chapter Twenty-Eight

Creation Story

The intergalactic alchemist and the interstellar scientist reached the point of creation and returned. Masters of time and space, their choices vast and decision fast, they chose Earth three hundred and thirty-three thousand years ago.

A fertile crescent between the Tigris and the Euphrates rivers lit, the appearance of seventy-two triangles flooded eastern Eden and illuminated the arriving reptiles. The solitary sovereigns to the throne of the Thirteen emerged from the matrix, stepped onto the ancient lands of Mesopotamia, and reached deep into the earth. From clay underfoot, the dark beings formed dark torches and breathed dark life into them.

The ancient reptilian beings, the sacred masculine and feminine held high their torches and called forth from the sky. Demonic flames awoke, apocalyptic embers tripped the light and the torchbearers summoned a third.

A solitary star shot through the realms to Earth, and through the inferno a blazing apparition emerged. A supernatural life force, the body of a man held in flight by fiery wings. The towering figure of Semyaza, lord of the Watchers, descended upon the Earth. The giant, once-divine being reached deep into the planet; from the wound he formed a torch, with his fire he created a trinity.

The torchbearers of dark fire and illumination cast their claim below and then skyward. The ceremonial flames lit the heavens and shadowed the Earth, and through the darkness, six stars awoke and trailed the path to Earth. The fallen Watchers of the angelic realms joined their leader, Semyaza, and the reptilian luminaries.

Nine primordial dark torchbearers now illuminated the grove and stood in sacred ceremony. In their wake and in their will, they called forth the infernal, the inverted, dark dimension jumpers.

Awoken from the fire, birthed from the smoke and fuelled by the ensuing sacred promise of an almighty parasitic invasion, the matrix delivered anarchy. Three Archons, daemons of the deep, joined the Order.

The growing conclave called out to the cosmos and summoned through spheres. They caught her midflight, once banished from the site, with one space remaining: Lilith, took up her righteous place.

A piccolo played as their karmic claim passed Jupiter's moons. The fire took hold and the thirteen torchbearers cast the flaming pentagram skyward. A ceremonial claim in time-honoured tradition, a declaration: war will be waged upon the heavens and the Earth if any stand in their way. The multiverse shuddered, the rains came early and a young man, positioned to witness, watched. The created Thirteen, set upon domination and destruction, disappeared into the matrix.

The observing hooded hermit laid down his stylus and held high the clay tablet. The indented etchings emitted vapours, streams of green light plunged towards the place the Order had formed. The light of the emerald tablet recorded the event: the creation of *The Prometheus Thirteen*.

Lightning Source UK Ltd.
Milton Keynes UK
UKHW010645270521
384461UK00002B/71